POTTY CHAMB

Copyright © Duncan Boyle, 2002

First published in 2002 on behalf of the author
by Scotforth Books,
Carnegie House,
Chatsworth Road,
Lancaster LA1 4SL,
England
Tel: +44(0)1524 840111
Fax: +44(0)1524 840222
email: carnegie@provider.co.uk
Publishing and book sales: www.carnegiepub.co.uk
Book production: www.wooof.net

All rights reserved.
Unauthorised duplication
contravenes existing laws.

British Library Cataloguing-in-Publication data
A catalogue record for this book is available
from the British Library

ISBN 1-904244-18-1

Typeset by Cambridge Photosetting Services, Cambridge
Printed and bound in the UK by Bookcraft (Bath) Ltd

POTTY CHAMBERS

by
Duncan Boyle

All characters in this work are fictional
and any resemblance to any persons living or dead is purely coincidental

SCOTFORTH BOOKS, 2002

To Anne with love for her patience and encouragement, and the other Anne for her sheer hard work and typing excellence.

CONTENTS

Piddletown	1
Tuesday Opening	2
Mr Smile	5
Mr Squeeze	9
Mr Quid	12
Mr Pickforth, Miss Treacle and Miss Bottoms	16
Miss Nockersby and Cashroom Staff	20
The Typists – and a Lucky Break	23
Mrs Mulcaster	26
Mr Snotty Rools O.K.	29
Miss Bottoms – Again	32
The Faculty Dinner	34
The Beginning	41
Duncan's Morning	45
Ogles and the Turds	48
Complaint	55
Beenie Gronnix	60
The Sermon	64
The Funeral	69
The Wedding	73
Après-Nuptials – The Monday following	81
Office Refurbishment	83
The Environmental Men	86
Signs of Summer – The Golf Outing	90
Friday the Thirteenth	92
Monday the Sixteenth	95
Bad Dreams – Still the Sixteenth	97
Tuesday the Seventeenth	102
Eleven O'clock Forenoon	104
Lunchtime	105
Afternoon	108

Wednesday the Eighteenth	111
Fiveskin – and Betty	125
Breathstone and Roxanne	130
Revd. Stella Cumming	135
The Rotary Lunch	138
The Open	141
The Latin Quarter	146
Indecent Exposure	148
The Hydro	151
Prospects of Partnership	167
The Christmas Spirit	172
Hogmanay	175
Epilogue	183

PIDDLETOWN

The rain swept in from the south-west on a bleak February in the nineteen seventies. In Piddletown, on the west of Scotland, the rain swept in from the south-west not only in February, and not only in the nineteen seventies, but for much of this and any other millennium. But the nineteen seventies were special, at least for those about whom these narratives are written. Their sense of fun, and their appreciation of their own not infrequent absurdities were largely untouched by bureaucratic interference. The eighties, and even more so the nineties, forced provincial lawyers, and their city counterparts to an even greater degree, to lose their smiles and cultivate instead the serious frowns of compliance and survival. Yes, the nineteen seventies were special.

This particular February, stuck on an ancient oaken pavement-side door at 41 Main Street, in addition to years of accumulated grime, is a tattered sign bearing the exciting news:

>   THIS OFFICE CLOSED on MONDAY
>   For LOCAL HOLIDAY
>   Re-opens 9 a.m. on Tuesday 5th.
>   H. CHANCER & CO
>   SOLICITORS.

The only persons to see the notice are a couple of school boys sheltering from the rain and an old lady, who stops to let her mongrel urinate against the empty milkbottle which had invited such attention since closing time on Friday. The wind and rain lasted all weekend, sealing Piddletown from the outside world, like a damp grey Brigadoon.

TUESDAY OPENING

8.50 a.m. The first of the three partners arriving at the Law Offices of Henry Chancer & Co climbs the damp tiled staircase, breathing in the scent of disinfectant pine. The cleaner's recent attack with mop and bucket has given an aura of 'public lavatory' to the surrounds. This is sharply overwhelmed in the first floor office proper by the acrid stench of stale tobacco, which has easily won the battle with furniture polish as the smell of the day.

Quite apart from the general staleness, dullness and untidiness, an outsider would be tempted to view that working conditions in such a place would, in the appropriate era, have had Charles Dickens rushing for his quill – or would even have given William Wilberforce something to chew on. Heavy iron bars block escape from all the rear windows, though only a fool would attempt to break in. To the front, facing the prevailing southwester from the sea down the road, the window frames are rotting and ill-fitting, and afford only scant protection from the elements. As with the premises of other people who grudge money on comprehensive modernisation, heating arrangements are variously by storage heaters, gas fires, coal fires, electric radiators, paraffin stoves – and a whole lot of hot air – most of which appliances continue to operate at full blast even in a heatwave, only then with the windows and door open. One year's fuel bill would more than pay the installation of central heating – if not the entire National Debt.

The first arrival, Mr Quid, is not the senior partner. The person with this doubtful privilege is an amiable buffoon, Mr Smile, and he is still in bed.

The third member of the firm, Mr Squeeze, will be at his desk at about 9.15 a.m. He'd probably be in later, but he has to drive his spoiled brats to the exclusive forest fringed neighbourhood private school. He doesn't really believe that his children will derive any benefit from private education, but his neighbours would have something to say about it if he got his kids educated on the cheap.

Tuesday Opening

Mr Quid has the morning mail opened by 9.15, by which time about half of the staff have just about honoured their contracts of employment, which call for a nine o'clock start. The telephone switchboard is quite busy after the long weekend, and its operator, Zoë Mulcaster, has had chances to engage her customary tact early on – such as:

'Mr Smile is not available at the moment – I'll get him to call you back when he's disengaged.'

This means that Mr Smile hasn't arrived, and is unlikely to show up this side of ten o'clock.

Mr Quid clicks on his dictating machine and whips through replies to correspondence, holding back for special attention anything of particular interest – nasty letters, complaints of inefficiency and the like – indeed, anything which looks like a challenge. His stated reason for a brisk start is that he is at his sharpest in the mornings. His real reason is that he's getting a spurt on as a compensation for his two-hour lunch and early afternoon departure home 'to beat the traffic'.

Mr Squeeze does not indulge himself with such hypocrisies. He reckons he's well worth his share of profits, and, having convinced himself of this, simply does his own thing.

Mr Smile says he comes in late because he performs best with a leisurely cooked breakfast inside him. Whether he performs best before, during or after breakfast – or at all – is his secret! In any event, as he says, 'I'm working long after everyone has sloped off at night.' In truth, he waits until he sees the tail-lights of Mr Squeeze's Rover out the Car Park, then he slopes off himself.

At 9.40 a.m. Miss Bottoms descends from her second floor hideout and stirs the loins of her audience by touring the office collecting dirty cups left over the weekend. For this ceremony, both partners present leave their doors open handsomely. In this way, they are the better positioned to catch a glimpse of the girl's sensuous walk as she glides past the opening. If law offices had piped music, this occasion would warrant a soft rendering of 'Cheek to Cheek'. This is the time of day when Messrs Squeeze and Quid take time off for a walkaround, stopping off at each vantage point en route.

Tea quite beautifully dispensed, Miss Bottoms commences her slow climb back to her sanctuary on the top deck, taking with her the eyes of Mr Smile, who is just arriving. What Mr Smile is thinking of is hard to tell, depending on what has, or has not, made him so late in arriving.

Some degree of normality is restored by 10.15 a.m. which is about as early as clients make appointments. Perhaps the consulters are as slow off the mark as the consultants. By this time Mr Quid's mail is on tape, and his typist Rachel is harnessed to her play-back machine, with her earphones giving her a stethoscope look. This is flattering her somewhat. The only doctor she resembles is Crippen, except that Crippen had a kindlier expression and a less convincing moustache.

Mr Squeeze won't have done too much about his dictation, knowing that his typist, Eunice, probably has a gigantic hangover, thus reckoning that it would be unwise to entrust her with anything important much this side of noon.

At 10.15 a.m. Mr Smile still hasn't looked at today's mail. It is doubtful if he's looked at Friday's mail, or at all that much of last week's mail. It's unkindly rumoured that he has unopened envelopes on his desk, sporting penny blacks! Says he's too busy to give attention to current work. And he probably believes it. A man of logic, Mr Smile is, albeit logic understood with less conviction by those clients who have suffered from his neglect. However, more of this later.

MR SMILE

Duncan Smile, Bachelor of Law. Aged 55, married to Doreen, five children, is built like a man for whom ready-to-wear suits are out of the question. Six feet two inches, pear-shaped, with one shoulder higher than the other, he is every bit a made-to-measure candidate. And with an inclination towards bright colours – but with no colour sense whatever – Duncan is identifiable from one end of town to the other in his garish yellow tweeds, usually garnished with stains. Former black hair is thinning and greying, his nose is roseate and prominent, and that which is most noticeable about his chin is its absence. Half moon glasses, chipped ill fitting teeth and frayed collars should complete the picture for you, along with suede hush-puppies which have seen better days.

A graduate of Edinburgh University, Duncan has one of these dialect free accents which suggest a hint of culture and this, coupled with his faded shabbiness generally persuades some people that he is a kind of 'gentry', and it's amazing how many clients he has acquired on the assumption that he is someone with those special attributes which ordinary mortals presume the nobility to have. However, in his frequent visits to the Ayrshire mining village in which he was born, especially when wearing his fishing gear, Duncan is accepted as the struggling yokel among struggling yokels. Blending in with whatever are his surroundings from time to time, Duncan is truly a man for all people, and held in regard for this reason, without it dawning on any of them that he isn't quite what he seems, as you'll discover.

Duncan Smile doesn't drink tea so his arrival in the mid-morning means coffee. As often as not, the coffee is on his desk in a lukewarm-to-set state when this lawyer arrives, briefcase in hand, to a room both warm and littered with papers ancient and modern – mostly ancient. Even the modern papers look ancient. Duncan's secretary (his partners only have typists) is one of these crawlers who is in sharp to attend to his gas fire and to make sure that everything is nice and cosy for her boss. Duncan shrugs his Army and Navy Stores nylon combat jacket off his ample shoulders with a weary sigh, demonstrative of the effort required for the operation – and clearly calling for a ten minute rest period. Duncan says he suffers from 'Executive Syndrome'. His efforts to describe what this means fall, for the most part, on deaf ears.

Zoë buzzes Duncan that 'There's a wee man in the waiting room in a tartan tammy who won't give his name, a stationery traveller called Malik, and an Insurance Inspector from the Provincial Temperance Society.'

'I'll give the swine Temperance,' muttered Duncan to himself absent-mindedly, and with positively no good reason.

The good lawyer shambled proudly to his huge blue diary and entered in green felt-tip for Tuesday 5th 'Engaged all morning'. He phoned Zoë and instructed that he'd take no calls till he'd cleared the waiting room of his keenly expected arrivals, but that he'd see the tartan tammy straight away.

As the tartan tammy entered, Duncan noisily slurped the remnants of his now cold coffee and opened the consultation.

'What is it today, then, Jock?'

Jock opened his coat, and beamed a toothless grin.

'What do you think of THAT, sir?' Jock enquired, looking downwards between his legs.

Duncan removed a worn plastic spec case from his frayed breast pocket, applied the lenses to his considerable nose, and peered at that which Jock held uneasily in both grubby hands.

'There'll be a good pound in that,' assessed Duncan, knowingly.

'Done,' shot Jock, picturing a large whisky on an imaginary bar counter.

Duncan peeled a crumpled oncer from the tapestry purse that he kept in his waistcoat, and exchanged it for the poke of hybrid golf balls that Jock had 'found' at Royal Titley Golf Course. Duncan didn't play golf that much, but reckoned that the two quid he'd get from his juniormost partner for the consignment was worth the one pound outlay. Well, isn't that what partnership is all about?

'Care for a wee drink of meths?' enquired the Tammy, producing a bottle of lilac fluid.

'Thank you, but no, my friend,' replied Duncan, patting his stomach. 'Doctor's orders, you know. No drinking before lunchtime. In any event, Jock, meths isn't my favourite tipple – no offence, mind – I'm sure it's very good.

'Well actually, sir, it's not my favourite either, but I can't afford twelve year old malt on the proceeds of the balls you buy.'

'Oh, here's another two nicker, mate – buy yourself a couple of decent Scotches. The meths will keep for another day'.

'God bless you, Mr Smile,' said Jock enthusiastically, grabbing the money, uncorking the meths, and finishing the bottle without a pause. 'Have to line my stomach before drinking whisky or I'll end up with a hangover!'

The Tammy winked, tossed the empty bottle just wide of Duncan's waste bucket, and searched the room for the way out.

Zoë isn't that good at remembering instructions, so by 10.40 a.m. Duncan had taken three phone calls – one from his wife to say she'd been locked out of the house, one from a Mr Gillick who had asked him to investigate the possibilities of buying the local Royal Hotel, presently for sale, and the third about a claim for compensation imminently at risk of being time-barred (if you don't know how serious this can be, ask a lawyer!)

Disturbed by the phone calls, Duncan forgot all about Malik and the Insurance Man till reminded by Zoë at 11.30 a.m. By the time Duncan had blethered with Malik, mostly about fly-fishing, and had seen the insurance chappie, he had forgotten all about Mr Gillick. He had also forgotten about his wife – but that was always easy, silly bitch! The compensation claim went completely out of his mind till prompted some months later by a letter from the Law Society wherein it was stated that –

'Your client, Mr Georgeson, complains that he instructed you to pursue his interest in the matter of a claim arising from serious injuries sustained at work some years ago, that you did nothing, that his claim is now time-barred, and that you told him it was all his fault for not reminding you often enough. Might your observations be respectfully forthcoming?'

Well, while Duncan wasn't thinking about Mr Gillick's hotel either, he *was* thinking of the local Law Society's Dinner this coming Friday at the

Savaloy Hotel. Duncan was to propose the vote of thanks, and was rehearsing his jokes. Pacing his room with tape-recorder in hand, he was oblivious to all else except the waves of imaginary applause, which assaulted his ears with deafening enthusiasm. He was so carried away with the adulation of the dress-suited hoard, that when he next looked at his watch, it was ten past two.

'Dammit,' Duncan muttered, 'I'll have to take things more easy or my bloody ulcer will play up.'

He popped a couple of blood pressure pills into his chinless mouth, and ambled heavily out to lunch.

'Nice day,' thought Duncan aloud. 'Think I'll walk – good for the old circulation.'

As he approached home, Duncan saw a green anorak and leopard-skin slacks hanging from the upstairs bathroom window-ledge, and his wife Doreen wearing the said garments and a very distraught look as the last scream she could muster passed her white lips.

'Shut up your moaning, woman,' shouted Duncan from a good hundred yards away, by no means quickening his step. As he drew near, Duncan leisurely selected the appropriate key from a bundle weighing two pounds, held it up towards his wife's bulging eyes, and instructed –

'Stop the acrobat stuff, Doreen. Open the door and serve lunch!' Doreen lost her grip on the ledge, toppled earthwards, and landed head-first into the very ripe compost heap. As she rose unaided to her feet, looking as if she had been soaked in treacle and straw, but smelling of something less appetising, Duncan opened the house door, 'hung' his coat on the hall floor, and shouted over his shoulder to the disconsolate Doreen – 'I suppose this means the red wine won't have been breathing the full hour, then, you stupid bitch!'

MR SQUEEZE

Raymond Squeeze, Honours Master of Arts, Bachelor of Laws, aged 49, married to Marjory, two children, for a while contemplated a career in the Church, but sensibly realised that his penchant for good living and bad language was unsuited to any pulpit.

Smarter in appearance than Duncan, if only just, Ray manages to get more years out of the one suit than is good for appearances, and for this and other 'careful' reasons has managed to acquire, as savings, a lot of money which should, one would think, be better spent than hoarded.

A single-figure handicap golfer, Ray carries a hint of snobbery about him, pleased to be associated with the 'Royal' Club of which he is a member and with those who, like himself, are among its chosen élite. But, like Duncan, Ray also can slip into his more modest past and relate to those who, deep down, are more his kin.

Ray is academically head and shoulders above the other two partners, a fact which is less than obvious when 'refreshed' in convivial company, by when it is extremely difficult to make sense of anything he says.

Five feet nine, twelve stones, fair thinning hair in need of a good wash, and the kind of shape to suggest that the occasional beverage is taken as a compliment to a sporting round of golf, Mr Squeeze's two handicap owes much to his assiduous application to the game. This renders his summer work schedule subject to unscheduled interruption. This man is more of a winter lawyer. Having said this, there's enough daylight even then to warrant a few holes, but the obsession is much more contained between October and April.

Ray's head jumped out from behind the morning paper at 10.20 a.m. when Zoë announced that there was a Mr Hansard in the Waiting Room talking about selling his house. Ray looked serious and said that if Mr Hansard could wait awhile, he'd see the gentleman shortly. As Zoë rang off, Ray allowed himself a smile and reached for the phone book to find that there were three Hansards listed. His eyes focused on 'HANSARD,

JOSHUA, TREETOPS.' Ray had heard that 'Treetops' is an £80,000–£100,000 property.

With a metaphorical rub of the hands, Ray's mental calculator rang up a minimum of £1,000 in sale commission and a conveyancing fee of not inconsiderable value as a bonus. Not bad by mid-morning on a wet Tuesday, and if Joshua was buying something elsewhere of commensurate value, then there's another good £1,000 in it.

Reaching for the intercom, and barely concealing his excitement, Ray invited Zoë to 'Send Mr Hansard in'.

Mr Hansard poked his nose apologetically into Ray's room, and, on being invited to be seated, fanned the plastic seat with his old cap, hitched up his mackintosh, hung his walking-stick on the edge of the adjacent book-case, and sat down, expelling a good three cubic feet of foul-smelling wind in the process.

Ray, with as much diplomacy as he could muster in the circumstances, edged himself towards the window and eased it up eighteen inches. Mr Hansard, not unconscious of the explosion of which he was guilty, removed his steamed-up steel rimmed glasses, rubbed his smarting eyes, and replaced the lenses on his bulbous red nose.

'What can I do for you, sir?' enquired Ray, his nostrils aiming for a shaft of outside air.

'I,eh, I, I w w want y you to to to s s s sell my my my h h house'.

Hansard had the most appalling stutter. Ray felt nervous. What with the thought of a fortune in the balance, that bloody awful smell, and that dreadful wee man keeping him waiting, Ray just *had* to take the initiative.

'Oh yes, Mr Hansard, that will be Treetops. I could come out to your beautiful home this afternoon to take particulars for advertising on my way back from the club – er, the court, I mean – when we can discuss details.'

'T-t-treetops?' struggled the wee man. 'I-I-I-I-l live in a f-f-flat in P-p-prison Street'.

Five minutes later, with hurried particulars taken of Hansard's flat – One rm., kit., & shrd toilet – Ray concluded the interview with as much composure as he had at his disposal.

'No need for me to inspect your flat, Mr Hansard – you have described it so very well.'

Mr Hansard collected his cap and his stick, farted voluminously, and left.

Ray dived for the window, gulped in a few lungfuls of air, and cursed the loss of two grand.

His head cleared, he phoned Miss Bottoms for a strong coffee. Ray's pulse began to race as he heard the slow tap of Miss Bottoms' heels – 'These bloody boots and tight jeans' he thought – 'God Almighty, it must be my age!' Quickly he forgot about Hansard and all other pestilential clients while he gaped at the coffee bearer's lope into and then out of the room, all as if in slow motion. The coffee helped a little, but the ruddy phone rang and burst into his lecherous reverie. As Ray yanked the phone from its mustard coloured cradle, the latter sailed on to the floor, and the contents of the near full cup splashed all over the front of his laterally creased trousers.

'Bugger it!' Ray snapped, as he espied the splintered case of the telephone on the carpet.

'Pardon?' enquired Zoë. 'That's Mrs Bell in for her 10.45 a.m. appointment.'

Ray muttered something unmentionable, thinking simultaneously about that dreadful Mrs Bell, and re-appraising the state of his trousers. Crossing his hands across his midriff like a fullback in a soccer 'wall', Ray made a beeline for the nearest washroom, and slammed and bolted the door. Feeling safe, he turned towards the washbasin – God! – Miss Bottoms was there already washing teacups. The girl's eyes took in the state of Ray's trousers, and smiled.

'No need to get *that* excited, Mr Squeeze – it is only coffee I serve.'

Diplomatically, and with an audible purr, the girl left Ray to his thoughts, and to his ablutions.

MR QUID

Jerry Quid, Bachelor of Law (Glasgow University – scraped through after re-sits) – aged 48, married to Anne, four children, five feet ten inches, looks thinner than he is, is the original jack of most trades but master of none. Well, maybe there is one for which he could receive an award, namely, acting the part.

Jerry arrived at Chancer's just weeks after Duncan, having been trained at one of Glasgow's most prominent law firms where he learned almost nothing except the need to be nice to everyone and to be liked in exchange. This facility endeared him to Henry Chancer, who made generous allowances for Jerry's many legal blind spots. What Jerry lacked in skill, he made up for with warmth, and thanks to the patience and tuition of Henry and Duncan – and of Raymond also when he joined the firm two years later – he acquired a passable understanding of the jobs he was paid to do, and by the time of Henry Chancer's death, Messrs Smile, Quid and Squeeze made a formidable team of practitioners, with a healthy connection of valued clients throughout the county.

So why is Jerry Quid the last to be referred to in this narrative? Well, it's mostly from his notes of the events about to be disclosed, that this book is written.

Jerome Lenza Quid, to give him his full name, used to be plain Jerry Quid till he was assumed into partnership. From working-class stock, he figured that using – or, even emphasising, his middle name might give his image a lift. With Italian ancestry on his mother's side (she was from Florence, and there was an Uncle Lorenzo), his parents' first thought had been to christen the lad Firenza – or even Lorenzo, for that matter. Compromise ruled Lenza the second string to Jerome, which was after his father. His father was a husky stevedore who thought the newborn was so 'puny' he should be called plain Florence, but his mother would have none of it.

Jerry is thin; showing traces of athleticism now choked out by sedentary breathlessness. Grey, bushy hair tops a hook-nosed angular face betraying his maternal ancestry. There is nothing of the stevedore about Jerry. Interest in the arts had long since displaced athletics that Tuesday morning. His mail dictated – even the awkward items – and his pulse recovered from Miss Bottoms' tea visit, Jerry swung his feet onto the desk and relaxed into sketching his office. His effort wasn't that good, as was evidenced by the use of more rubber than lead. When Zoë announced the arrival of a Mr Cueball, Jerry's feet arced to the floor in a well-practised fashion, and he ushered the client to a seat with the flamboyance of a magician.

It transpired that Mr Cueball sought divorce. It was narrated by the gent that his wife had been unfaithful with a Mr Green, and had finally left home with a Mr Black. Jerry, being a snooker enthusiast, ventured the observation that Mr Black looked the more permanent paramour at odds of seven to three. Mr Cueball didn't even smile at the tactless suggestion.

'What evidence can you produce to support your assertion that your wife has committed adultery?' enquired Jerry.

'Do what?' Cueball looked baffled.

'How can you prove that Mrs Cueball has been, er, having if off?' Jerry clarified.

''Cos I bloody caught them, that's how,' came the riposte.

'Is there independent testimony?' Jerry asked slowly and deliberately, as if talking to an Irishman – 'any independent testimony – you know – did anyone witness the occurrence?'

'Not till the bloody negative is enlarged,' Cueball replied

'Oh, I see,' said Jerry. 'They posed for it, did they?'

'Don't be so dampt facetious, Mr Quid. I suspected my wife was at it, so I got my camera, burst into the bedroom, and took the picture.'

'A quick flash?' Jerry asked, innocently.

'Too bloody true they were,' Cueball thundered, and threw a foolscap envelope on Jerry's desk. A strip of negatives fell out, and Jerry, lifting it gingerly so as neither to contaminate nor be contaminated, held the specimen up to the light, and sucked in audibly.

'I see,' said Jerry, simply, and to the point.

'Too bloody right you see,' seethed Cueball.

'Is this Green or Black?' asked Jerry, composing himself.

'No, it's black and white, but if you're getting it tinted, the wife's hair is blue,' came the gormless reply.

Seeing there was enough evidence – or, at least the makings of something interesting – Jerry invited Cueball to leave the negatives for processing and advised his client that a report would be sent on the prospects for divorce once counsel had been brought in. Cueball seemed satisfied, and made an appointment for three weeks hence

Quid's next appointment disturbed his reverie about a deserted tropical beach. Finding himself faced by farmer Torquil Monacle Esq., and that Mr Monacle had been charged with stealing sheep from his neighbour's farm, Jerry took a studious look at the crumpled summons which his client dropped on the desk. Actually, he didn't look at it all that carefully, because Jerry didn't do criminal work, or know all that much about it.

'Nasty,' whispered Jerry, lighting a fag. 'Tell you what I'll do, Mr Monacle – I'll take you to see our court man – couldn't put you in better hands.....very well respected he is by all the judges. A man who'll give you straight honest advice.'

'I don't want straight honest advice, laddie,' shouted Monacle. 'I want to get off!'

'You mean, Mr Monacle, to plead 'Not Guilty' and to have the matter tried and decided by the fair and impartial decision of the Court?'

'Bloody Hell, man – I said no such thing. I INSIST that you get me off. Now SEE TO IT, and less of all that crap you lawyers talk. SEE TO IT!!' the farmer repeated, and swayed out.

Bet he's guilty as Hell, thought Jerry to himself, fumbling for his cigarettes. Ruddy farmers are always up to something.

The summons was passed to Farquhar Pickforth, Court Assistant extraordinaire.

Twenty minutes later, Farquhar appeared in Jerry's room.

'Did you look at what was stapled to the back of the Summons, Mr Quid?' he postulated.

Only *very* young lawyers postulate, or silly older ones struggling to impress.

Jerry shook his head laterally without raising his eyes from a holiday brochure.

'That Mr Monacle – nice man,' continued Farquhar, 'has five previous convictions for malicious mischief, all involving the next farm. Seems there's some kind of running battle between the two of them. His neighbour probably has a record as well, stupid twits that they are.'

'A long-playing record, perhaps,' muttered Quid absentmindedly, waving Farquhar towards the door, and continuing his studies, the atmosphere now blue with tension-induced smoke.

Farquhar rubbed his smarting eyes as he left, went to the Gents for a glass of water, and the consequences of the same.

MR PICKFORTH, MISS TREACLE AND MISS BOTTOMS

Farquhar took the summons upstairs to his attic office, phoned a mate of his at the Prosecutor's Office, and learned that his guess about the Monacle man was correct. Mr Monacle farmed Gledhills, 450 acres mixed arable, pasture and woodland. His next neighbour was one Jason McTough who farmed Easter Gledhills, only marginally smaller. Part of the boundary between the two passed through a plantation of pine and spruce. There had been a history of aggro there, variously taking the form of encroachment, diversion of water supplies, fence-cutting and similar instances of 'accidental' damage. Stock wandering east to west and vice versa had become commonplace through breached walls, hedges and fences. The police knew all about the situation but turned a blind eye so far as possible. But in this instance, Farmer McTough had insisted on 'pressing charges'.

Farquhar, flushed with the importance (to him, anyway) of the information he had gleaned, set off downstairs to impress Mr Quid with the high level of his application to duty.

Jerry had gone to lunch.

Farquhar, deflated, tried the door handle of the office next to Jerry's. Miss Lotte Treacle, two years Farquhar's senior at twenty-eight sat demurely at her desk and raised her dark eyes seductively as he entered. She listened patiently as Farquhar told her of the Monacle affair, then stood up, smoothed down her navy skirt with long, slim fingers tipped with beautifully manicured nails, brushed her dark hair with her hand – obviously very conscious of her appearance and quite obsessive about good grooming.

'Bother,' she said, 'Mr Squeeze has been consulted by McTough, and I have been asked to take charge of an action for damages against Mr Monacle. You'll have to tell Monacle to get another lawyer. We can't act for them both – conflict of interest, you know,' she explained, flexing a bit of intellectual muscle on her junior.

'They've both got a bob or two,' replied Pickforth, showing uncharacteristic loyalty of law assistant to employer. 'I shouldn't imagine either Squeeze or Quid would want to jettison a wealthy client'.

'That's their problem, not ours,' shrugged Lotte. 'Let's tell them the good news this afternoon. That should have the fur flying! But for now, Farquh, I thought you were taking me out for a bite?'

'Great,' responded Farquhar. 'Shall we eat before or after?'

Lotte pretended not to hear, and left to powder her nose.

By three-fifteen, it had been possible for Lotte and Farquhar to get Quid and Squeeze together with them in Ray's Office. Farquhar led off, explaining the dilemma.

'Like Hell I will,' barked Jerry. 'Monacle has a bigger farm, more cash, a heart condition, no relatives and I am sole Executor if he snuffs it. He's made more than one reference to selling Gledhills. He's too valuable to lose.'

Jerry's argument was totally watertight to any greedy lawyer. Ray, though fitting this description to a 'T' without the use of makeup, took a professional stance –

'McTough came to see me first – before your man showed up – first come, first served. So, get this much clear, *Mister* Quid, this firm is acting for McTough, and how you sort out *your* problem, matey, is up to you.'

Jerry made to respond, but Ray captured the moment, and held on –

'My position is clear. I won't change my mind, Mr Quid, so save your frigging breath!'

'Crap!' yelled Quid, made for the door, and slammed it decisively on the three of them. Jerry aimed for his room, wheeled round the corner preceding his doorway, and whacked into Miss Bottoms squarely, if not altogether fairly. Apologies exchanged, Jerry breathed in sharp and deep, and felt better with uncanny immediacy.

Ray Squeeze felt better too. Left with two young assistants to impress – and one of these a nubile female to boot – he lent back on his chair, swivelling to and fro, beaming.

'No point in beating about the bush,' he pontificated. 'I wasn't being bloody-minded with Mr Quid. First come, first served – that's the rule.

Mr Quid may smart at the thought, but he'll have to send his Monacle elsewhere. If he can do that *and* keep the connection, good for him – and for us. But Monacle won't be overjoyed that his loathed neighbour has engaged Monacle's own lawyers to set about him, will he?'

Ray waved the impressed youngsters away, and then indulged in a few thoughts on the economic considerations of the situation. He lifted the phone, and told Zoë to get him McTough. He was put through so quickly that it was a fair guess that McTough was not at the far end of the farm when his phone rang.

'Look, Jason,' launched Ray. 'What's all this junk about you and Monacle, *again*! The two of you are acting the silly bugger, and I'm having no part in it. Let me call off the dogs, tell the Prosecutor that your bloody beasts strayed – and golf with me at the weekend – how about it?'

McTough huffed and he puffed, and then he yielded to the advice of his lawyer, and accepted the invitation to golf. Ray squared things with the Prosecutor, then phoned Monacle, stating that he was doing so on behalf of Mr Jerome Quid, who was 'engaged out of the Office all day.'

'If,' Ray said to Monacle – '*If* the sheep stray back to Easter Gledhills fairly quickly, there will be no prosecution.'

Monacle took the hint.

At 9.30 a.m. the following day, Wednesday, a surprised Jerry saw Monacle enter his room and sit himself down.

'I've had enough bloody farming,' bellowed Torquil. 'Sell the damn place!'

Jerry, not knowing of Ray's decisive string-pulling of the previous afternoon, simulated a calm understanding of his client's instruction, said all the right things, made all the right gestures and murmurings, promised to visit the farm on Friday morning, and sighed in almighty relief as he heard the farmer's big boots echo in the stairwell, leaving for the street outside. First priority was to tell Ray, who swung on his chair with a particularly smug grin.

'This calls for a celebration,' Ray chuckled, as he phoned to solicit two coffees from Miss Bottoms.

'I could get the coffees myself,' continued Ray. 'But I much prefer room service, don't you?' Ray winked.

'By the way' – still Ray – 'You'll know that McTough is letting your old rascal off the hook *and* the Prosecutor's dropping charges.'

'How the Hell do you know that?' Jerry shot out.

Ray tapped the side of his nose.

'A little birdie, matey – and I'll tell you more – Jason McTough told me a month ago he'd pay £200,000 for your Monacle's place if it came on the market – sound him out, and make us all a few grand.'

Miss Bottoms knocked, and entered slowly with a coffee in each hand, gently laying each on a spare gap on Ray's cluttered desk.

'Be a dear, Miss Bottoms,' said Ray. 'Get me James Young's file from the cabinet.'

Two pairs of eyes followed the girl to the filing cabinet, and watched carefully as she stretched her jeans, bending to the bottom right-hand drawer. Virginia fumbled among the tatty brown folders and eventually came up with the file, which she handed to Ray before turning for the door.

'Many thanks indeed,' said Ray with total sincerity.

When the girl had gone, Ray put Mr Young's file right back from whence it had been taken.

'Could have asked for Alex Abram's file, Jerry, but it's more fun watching her bending!'

MISS NOCKERSBY AND CASHROOM STAFF

The cash department in any law office is a place apart. It's a kind of engine room. The ship would float without it, but it couldn't go forwards without it – or backwards for that matter.

Miss Nockersby had been cashier for twenty-five years. She had looked all of fifty-four years when she arrived all these years ago. She still looked fifty-four. The difference was she now was fifty-four. She did everything with a meticulous attention to detail, and frequently attacked her employers with disdain about their lack of acumen in money matters – usually with a fair measure of justification.

She arrived daily at about 9.10 a.m., by which time Miss McScuddy has the Cash Room 'sorted out' for the day's work. Mrs Plum, a retired widow of ample dimensions, waddled in on the cashier's heels, and strained her iron coat-peg to the point of discomfort as she disrobed for business. Among her morning mail, Yolande Nockersby found bills for stationery, office equipment, property advertising charges, some land rent and insurance premium cheques, mortgage remittances, orders and cash in payment of accounts rendered, and all manner of banking and associated money matters. She had a list of Fee Notes and Accounts for services rendered to send out, some for work done and some for work hardly done at all. She knew which was which. In brief, her work was a whole bundle of laughs! Having said this, the economic welfare of Messrs Chancer depended on Yolande's knack, and the backup she received from Mesdames McScuddy and Plum, the former of which presided over the electronic accounting machine like a theatre organist of yore. The Partners placed total reliance on the expertise of this trio, and with good reason for their confidence. It also enabled the partners themselves to be sloppy, which they probably would be anyway.

Lotte Treacle had just completed a house sale deal for Duncan, and wafted into Yolande's Cash Factory with a sale statement and the cheque received from the purchaser's solicitor. Miss Treacle stood to elegant attention as the venerable cashier adjusted her glasses and ran her well-scrubbed fingers over the various items in the statement.

'Who prepared this statement, Miss Treacle?' enquired Yolande.

'Mr Smile, Miss,' came the relieved reply. Lotte smelled trouble.

'I thought as much,' snapped the cashier, 'That man couldn't add up a three item grocery bill – *look at this* ... see lawyers!!... It says "*add interest to compensate seller for delay in completion*" and that stupid man has *subtracted* it. How on earth is anything supposed to balance in this place? *leave this to me*, Miss Treacle!'

Yolande was enjoying this as only a cashier can do – or maybe a G.P.O. Counter assistant, or a teacher – a kind of masochistic pleasure, which such people indulge in, snapping at the persons nearest to hand, just for the release of tension.

The cashier marched purposefully towards the room of the unsuspecting Duncan, brushing Miss Treacle aside as if she were a cobweb. Miss Nockersby knocked on Duncan's door and barged in simultaneously. Duncan had his back to the door, and was laughing out loud at something he had just thought of. Before that, he had been busy making up a batch of family films in order to send them off to Kodak for processing with the office mail. On hearing the cashier's strident entry, Duncan wiped the tears of good humour from his eyes with a filthy tissue, and enquired

'What's the matter, Miss Knockersby?'

The lady didn't reply, but threw the Statement on Duncan's cluttered desk.

Duncan fumbled for his specs, and peered at the statement, picking his teeth with a pencil.

'What the hell if the client's name *is* spelt wrong?' thundered Duncan. 'The cheque will be made out to *us*, won't it, woman?'

He flicked the Statement back towards Yolande, gloating in his quick spotting of an obvious error.

'*Mr Smile*!' Throwing the Statement back – '*Add* these two figures, Please!'

Duncan searched for his calculator. He did nothing without a mechanical aid. He poked a few digits with his bitten forefinger. Spotting the more relevant mistake, he responded like all persons who would rather commit suicide than apologise.

'Now look here, Miss Nockersby, I made up this statement at the end of an all-night work session when all you lot were asleep. I was that blooming tired trying to make your living for you that some piddling mistake was bound to happen. Now just correct it, Miss Nockersby – that's what you're paid for. Don't come whining to me – I have more important things to do!'

Yolande melted into tears, and, muttering something about her 'notice', left Duncan's room chastened.

Duncan phoned through to Lotte and chewed her off for failing to check his work properly. Lotte wept at Duncan's sharp reprimand. As for Duncan, he went to the loo, and sat for ten minutes counting the tiles on the wall. This, and other things, done the lawyer returned to his room and summoned the cashier. He made as fulsome apology as he was capable of muttering, all the while looking out of the window, and telling her of how ill he was feeling whilst ostentatiously swallowing three pills in slow motion to substantiate his claim to ill-health, overwork and worry. He also offered the lady a substantial increase in salary if she'd agree to stay with the firm, swallowing nervously all the while.

Peace was restored – at a price.

THE TYPISTS – AND A LUCKY BREAK

The typists at Chancers' Law Office occupied two rooms on the top floor. There had been comings and goings over the years – marriages and pregnancies, frequently in that order – and other causations of departure prompting the need for new blood.

Chi-Chi, Rachel and Ethel shared the southern most room, and Sandy, Eunice and Darky the other. It's as well that the rooms were of identical shape and size, or they'd have argued about that too, as well as about everything else. Ray monopolised the skills of Chi-Chi and Sandy – and of Eunice on the odd day she might be up to it. Duncan used Darky (the creep) and a bit of Ethel. Ethel, however, suffered from a chronic, heady body-odour, so Duncan's dealings with her were mostly by phone or messenger. Jerry had Rachel to himself, and Lotte and Farquhar 'shared' Eunice more and more as Ray called upon her less and less.

Ethel and Eunice were great buddies and pals. The smells of stale whisky and B.O. seemed to cancel each other out to the extent that neither lady found the other offensive.

Eunice in particular is a bonny sight in the mornings when her typewriter's principal use is to support her head. She'd have been fired long since, but it's not easy to get shot of staff nowadays. Furthermore, she's a superb typist when in the mood – and what do you expect for fifty quid a week anyway? It was a different reason that kept Ethel in her job – no one was prepared to go near enough to initiate the required warning procedures which serve as a prerequisite to dismissal! And again, since her room-mates are unenthusiastic about socialising with poor Ethel, they all get on with their work with less interruption.

It was Sandy, however, who was sitting, knees together, notepad and pencil in hand, facing her 'boss' Ray, when the phone rang. Hearing that Mrs Gow was on the line, Ray cursed, but invited Zoë to 'Put Mrs Gow through'.

'How nice to hear from you, Mrs Gow. I hope you are keeping most well,' lied Ray. 'I was just on the point of phoning you with good news.'

In fact, Ray had found it very easy indeed to forget all about Mrs Gow's petty business.

'Good news, is it?' replied the old bag.

'Yes indeed. Your brother has decided *not* to contest Auntie Jessie's will, so it looks like you'll inherit the lot.

'I don't know if I like it,' Mrs Gow replied, her brain clicking into suspicious place. 'Indeed, I *don't* like it one little bit,' she continued. 'That swine must be up to something!'

Brotherly love exuded from Mrs Gow's voice.

'Well,' rejoined Ray, 'He did say something about if he got some clock or another as a memento of his dear aunt, then that would suffice.'

'A clock, is it!' the lady burst. 'His dear aunt, is it! – well, Mister Squeeze, I don't know about any clock, but get it bloody valued before that bastard gets his mitts on it!'

'Very well, Mistress Gow,' tremored Ray, hoping like hell that Pickforth hadn't lent out Auntie's keys so that the brother could say farewell to the place which 'had been like a second home to me' – as the brother had emotionally described it, or piffle to this effect.

A dash across to Pickforth's room, and Ray's hope was dashed.

Half an hour later, Pickforth phoned Ray from Auntie Jessie's house.

'There's no clock here, Mr Squeeze – just a badly written note stuck to the mantelpiece next the dust-free square where a clock has probably stood till very recently. The note says 'Thanks, Mate'.'

'Get on to the police straightaway, Farquhar, and report a burglary,' snapped Ray.

'With respect, sir', replied Farquhar, '*we* gave out the keys – doesn't that make US responsible?'

'*Us* responsible? *Us*?? Shouted Ray. 'It was *you* who gave out the bloody keys. Get back here at once!'

Ray slammed down the phone, and thought a moment or two. Right enough, blaming Mr Pickforth might ease his tension, but he, Ray, was the man accountable. The buck stopped with Messrs Chancer – or the Indemnity Insurers as something of a last resort.

Ray checked on Aunt Jessie's file, and made a note regarding Mrs

Gow's brother – name of Cyrus Finch, 27 Breadalbane Close. Lumme! – Lotte Treacle lives at number 29!

Ray got to his revived feet, put on his most sympathy-inducing face, crossed to Miss Treacle's door, knocked gently, and waited till called.

'I wouldn't normally wish to impose on you, Lotte, but could I ask you for a favour?'

Lotte betrayed none of her suspicion as she expressed her willingness to help.

'Could I trouble you to look in on Mr Finch on your way home – in fact you can leave early – even now, maybe, if you're clear – and ask Mr Finch what he knows about his Auntie Jessie's clock.'

'His Auntie Jessie's clock?'

'Yes, Lotte, Just that – note his reply, and tell me in the morning, please.'

Next forenoon, Miss Treacle struggled up the stair with the ugliest looking timepiece that Ray had ever clapped eyes on. A scratched walnut monster with mahogany and ivory inlay about two feet high.

'How did you manage that, you clever girl?' beamed Ray.

Miss Treacle deposited the article, smoothed her clothes, and patted the back of her hair.

'Mr Finch said he'd got all he wanted from the clock, and that I was welcome to it.'

Ray thought – for the second time that week.

'You mean, there was something valuable – money maybe – hidden inside?'

'He didn't say so in as many words, but I think that's what he meant,' Lotte was enjoying playing sleuth.

'Good girl – thanks,' said Ray with relief, and watched her leave. Nice girl thought Ray – a lot of thinking for one week. Good looking too. He rang Miss Bottoms for two coffees and buzzed Jerry for company and a gloat. After all, Cyrus had got his cash, and Ray had the clock with which to satisfy Mrs Gow. And in any event, Mrs Gow was a conniving bitch who deserved as much as she got – or as little.

MRS MULCASTER

'Sorry, Mr Quid, I thought you said 268257'

'Decidedly not, Zoë, I said 262857'

'Sorry again, Mr Quid, I'll try to get it right this time.'

'Stupid woman,' muttered Jerry. Fancy having a telephonist who gets all confused with numbers. In fairness she usually gets the right numbers. It was just that she put them in the wrong order.

His phone rang its shrill ring.

'Hello.'

'That's Mr Monacle now, Mr Quid – I'll put you through.'

'Hello, Quid. Now, about the sale of Gledhills, I want a quarter of a million – and I'll accept an offer from anyone *but* McTough.'

'Surely, Mr Monacle, McTough's money is as good as anyone else's?'

'Look Quid, it's *my* place – and I'd rather give it away than sell it to McTough for a million!'

Liar – and, what's more, a liar who's unconscious of a lawyer's need to make an extravagant living.

'Very well, Mr Monacle – I'll see you Friday.'

'Be here!' spat Monacle, as he slammed off.

Funny, thought Jerry, how a man can derive such satisfaction from being in a state of constant anger. However, human nature is a fickle spirit, and filthy lucre plays a bigger role in a man's decisions than he would admit – even to himself. Specially if the man has plenty of the stuff to gain – or to lose!

It was no surprise to Jerry when he drove into the yard at Gledhills on Friday to find Monacle and McTough, arms linked, emerging from the byre.

'Get it put in writing, Quid – sold to McTough at £180,000 – and no commission to you for selling, mind. I sold it myself, remember, and at a damn sight more than your bloody lot would have got for me. Oh – *plus* stock, equipment and crops at valuation – *and* something for un-exhausted manures – *and* I want out of here a week from today with my money in my hand – *and no* Capital Gains Tax, mind.'

McTough nodded agreement to those elements relevant to his interest, each spat some greenish slime on his outstretched right hand, then both his and Monacle's hands splashed into each other enthusiastically.

'Bloody Hell,' thought Jerry. 'Trust a friggin' farmer – sets you an impossible task, and sure as guns will fall out with you if the miracle doesn't happen as directed – and not even a Whitsun or Martinmas takeover to give some time for the formalities! Twice the work in a fraction of the time – and no bloody commission. The 'No Capital Gains Tax' bit, however, represents good news. We'll get a good screw just keeping him out of jail!' Jerry hated having to work for his fees, but if a client – especially a wealthy farmer – sought to sell him short, be sure (thought Jerry) there are avenues through which to be compensated.

When he got back from Gledhills, Jerry got three messages from Mrs Mulcaster. One of the messages was right, one was nearly right, and one was positively wrong. The important message was the fourth one, which she forgot to mention at all. He learned about that one at 4.30 p.m. when he was about to leave for home. It was a phone call from the General Hospital.

'Staff Nurse Croxley here, Mr Quid – don't bother to come now; Mrs Henshaw has just died'.

'Oh, I am sorry,' said Jerry, puzzled. 'I'll get in touch with her son right away.' And he replaced the receiver, and lit a fag.

The smoke did nothing to calm him, and, throwing the cigarette into his pail-sized ashtray, Jerry thundered out his room to the switchboard, and yelled –

'MRS MULCASTER! What's this about my having been called to the hospital?'

'Oh yes, Mr Quid – a Mrs Benlaw wants to make her will. She's none too well, I believe'.

'Mrs *Henshaw*, you idiot, couldn't live long enough for you to give me the message!'

Without waiting for either tears or an apology, Jerry slammed himself back into his room and dialled Louie Henshaw himself on his private line, thinking whilst waiting that if he had asked the Mulcaster woman to do it for him, he'd probably have been put through to a Pub or a Bookmakers.

Louie answered the phone eventually, and Jerry apologised for having been out of town on business during the old lady's concluding crisis.

'Not at all, old boy,' replied Louie cheerily. 'The old girl was planning to leave her estate to the Cats Home, so your absence was a real Godsend.'

God works in a mysterious way, thought Jerry.

MR SNOTTY ROOLS O.K.

Mr Paul Snotty hardly merited the 'Mister'. He was barely five feet three, with ginger hair and a pink unshaved face still in the throes of acne. Apprentice lawyer he might be, but of appearance more akin to that of the traditional office boy, and treated accordingly.

His room – more like a walk-in cupboard – faces the Ladies' 'restroom' on the top deck, where the tea was made, dishes washed, and where the female loos were housed. Paul's door is never shut. Day by day, little by little, he was learning a bit about legal practice, and a whacking great deal about the female staff. He of all people knew most of how much, and how little, work was done on 'his' floor. Paul thought of his zone as a beehive. The bees spent some of their time elsewhere, but they always found their way back to the rest room as if regular visits there were vital to their very lives. They probably were.

Paul was a very studious apprentice lecher; well versed on who was going to the toilet, who has just been, and exactly for what purpose. Snotty had been at a boys' school, had no sisters, and found himself disturbed and curious in almost exclusively female confines. None of the females spoke to Mr Snotty unless they had to. And they didn't often have to.

Farquhar and Lotte used Snotty as their dogsbody.

On Friday morning, when Jerry was at Gledhills, Paul was in Mr Quid's room, playing at lawyers, feet on desk, and swivelling around in his master's chair. Mr Quid's room was right next to the Reception area, and the odd client who didn't know the ropes about reporting at the desk, and failing to notice the 'Enquiries' sign on the counter, wandered straight into Jerry's room on the strength of his nameplate on the door.

One such found himself in Jerry's doorway while Paul was at play.

'Ah huvnae an appointment, but can youse see me noo, son? It's awful important.' A yobbo in his early twenties, the gent in the doorway towered over the blushing trainee, flicking the earring which dangled from his left auricle as if the pierce-hole had gone septic – which was by no means impossible taking into account the state of him otherwise. Paul was short on neither cheek nor enterprise, and, in any event, wasn't this the time to learn?

Paul flicked one of Jerry's fags out of the ever-ready packet, lit up, coughed uneasily, and proffered the packet to 'his' client.

'Naw, Jimmy – ah roll ma ain.'

'Er, sit down, sir,' invited Paul, flushing with excitement. 'What is it we can do for you?'

'Ah've been done for serious assault, Mister –?'

'Snotty,' helped Paul. 'I think we should get a few details.'

Paul found some blank foolscap and a biro, and took notes from the gentleman's dictation, translating as he went into something nearer English. The notes read –

'Charles Leonard Grateman, Labourer (unemployed) of 3A Dell Lane. Aged 27 years (looks younger). Single. Was walking his greyhound along the harbour wall at 3 a.m. on Wednesday 23rd when four huge men stopped their navy blue Escort and set about him with their fists'.

Grateman stopped, and Paul looked up enquiringly, stubbing out his fag with relief.

'I thought you said *you* were being charged?'

'Well, ah hud tae defend masel' an' ma dug – it's a guid dug, ken, an' ah wisnae tae jalouse that thae bruisers wis polis, wis ah?'

'Didn't the officers exchange words with you before the fisticuffs?'

'Whit's that, ken?' puzzled Charles.

'Surely, Mr Grateman, the policemen didn't just jump you and thump you without saying anything?'

'Well, ah think wan o' them said somethin' aboot stuff nicked frae a ship, or somethin'.'

'Did you find out what it was that had been nicked?'

Snotty thought he was doing quite well.

'Ah hardly ken masel', Jimmy – ah hud tae chuck it ower re side when ah seen ra polis comin'.'

'So you KNEW they were police?'

'Ah ken noo – that's all youse need tae pit doon in yer notes, son.

Foreby, ah'm no' charged wi' theft – ah wis only helpin' ra polis wi' thur enquiries – an' they done me in therr an' then.'

'Do you want me to make a complaint for you, Mr Grateman?'

'If ra polis go ahead wi' thur assault charge, ah waant them done an' a'. Efter a', ah wis kep in jug a' nicht, an' ma dug didnae like it neithers!'

'Have you received a summons – you know – a typed sheet with details of the charge?'

'Ah goat that when ah wis in Court this morning,' quoth Charles, pulling grubby crumpled papers from his tartan donkey jacket. 'Ah pled 'No' Guilty' an' baillt masel oot, ken, wi' a wee windfall ah hud frae ra gee-gees yesterday.'

Taking the summons from Mr Grateman, Paul invited that the matter be left in his capable hands, and showed his new client to the exit with a reluctant handshake.

'Whew!' thought Paul, as he re-slumped into Jerry's chair. 'Double whew!' he thought further as his eyes scanned the long list of previous convictions.

'Triple whew!' Paul exclaimed aloud as he noticed that his watch had been skilfully detached from his wrist.

Snotty dialled Miss Bottoms.

'Coffee for Mr Quid's room, please.'

'Get stuffed, Snotty,' the girl screeched – 'Quid's out – get your own bloody coffee!'

Well, elation is usually short-lived for the humble as well as for the proud.

MISS BOTTOMS – AGAIN

Virginia Bottoms (Miss) joined the Firm on leaving School. Her father had pled with Duncan to give his daughter a chance. She had three 'O' Levels, right enough, but at the lower end of each, and in three of the less academic fields of endeavour. Had there been exams for preening, sensuality and precociousness, nothing less that 'A' Levels with distinction would have adorned the girl's scholastic diploma.

Virginia would get by. She had the aptitude of being chosen whilst better candidates faltered. Miss Bottoms, in the vernacular, had what it takes. Her father's pleadings on her behalf to Duncan were wholly unnecessary – specially to someone like Duncan. Duncan had her hired on reputation and appearance alone, and would have promoted her within the week had it not been for the restraining influence of what little sense he had.

Miss Bottoms was engaged to perform general and the most basic of office chores. Even on those many occasions when she did positively nothing, her employers reckoned her worth every penny. Each of Smile, Quid and Squeeze had a minor seizure, at least daily, at the slightest thought that she might leave, even some day in the future. They could get another assistant, another typist – even another partner – but never another Miss Bottoms. Whether Miss Bottoms was late, over-lunched – or went 'missing' for a couple of hours or more – no one would chastise her. Miss Bottoms had it made – and she knew it!

Mr Smile was working late well into the night on the Thursday evening immediately preceding the Law Society's Dinner the day following. Well, till about 5.15 p.m. Miss Bottoms slid through his open door without knocking.

'Is there anything you want before I go, sir?' she enquired, waking Mr Smile from his reverie.

Duncan nearly swallowed his ballpoint pen, and reached for his blood-pressure pills.

'Pardon? – ahem,' Duncan stuttered, removing his glasses to wipe the gathering steam. 'Could you perhaps baby-sit for me tonight. My good lady wife is away from home overnight, and I shall be housebound without a minder.'

'But you don't have any babies, sir!'

'I'll borrow some, if that'll make any difference.' Quite clever, smiled Duncan to himself, his head lowered.

Virginia fluttered her long lashes, walked hungrily round to Duncan's side of the desk and stood alarmingly close so that he had to rub his eyes just to focus on her lovely upturned face.

Miss Bottoms smiled warmly, and then her face – frame by frame as if in slow motion – hardened grotesquely and her pale blue eyes turned jet black.

'Get lost, fatso!' she yelled, as her right hand connected with Duncan's cheek, sending his glasses spinning into the waste-bucket.

As the girl whirled round and stamped out of Duncan's room, the chastened lawyer mouthed 'You're fired' but nothing audible passed his ashen lips.

He wouldn't dare.

THE FACULTY DINNER

There is always a buzz of expectancy on the Friday when the lawyers in the district are due to congregate for their Annual Dinner. All solicitors – with rare exceptions, which don't concern us – are members of the Law Society. Local groups of solicitors have their own 'club within the Club', frequently called 'The Faculty of Solicitors', and that whether or not all or any of the members are truly in possession of their faculties! The lawyers at Messrs Chancer and their local colleagues will throng tonight at the Savaloy Hotel for their annual occasion – about forty of them, but with guests making up the numbers to nearer one hundred and thirty. It's a night for anticipation, self-aggrandisement and nostalgia.

Anticipation is in the hearts of the young, with visions of advancement in the profession. Conceited self-aggrandisement is the mark of flamboyant middle-age among those who *think* they've made it. Nostalgia among the older members has them looking back on earlier dinners with fond recall of those 'no longer with us'. Of course, the recall is fond only because the old buggers are now dead. There's usually a holiday style atmosphere in the office on dinner day.

Jerry missed out on this because he was out of the office for most of the day. Duncan was engrossed in the preparation of the concluding gems for his speech – and avoiding Miss Bottoms. Ray was left to fix up the dinner-table arrangements, and the orders for wines and spirits. This last job gave Ray particular pleasure. Farquhar was eager to help, because he had been invited to attend, and this was to be his first taste of the big time. At ten past five, Miss Nockersby was the only person left in the office. Her light continued to burn till her enthusiastic pen ran dry at 6.36 p.m.

By then, the partners and Farquhar were straightening their bow-ties in their respective homes before being driven to the hotel, there to rendezvous with their guests at seven o'clock. The guests of Messrs Chancer this year were the man from the Building Society, Bert Squeeres, Bank Manager J. Bawll Braynes, Insurance Inspector Callum Cotterill, and Messenger-at-Arms Sid Stones. A table for eight.

Large spirit glasses in hand, Jerry with the inevitable fag, and Ray indulging a large cigar 'for that special occasion', the usual proliferation of inconsequential clap-trap filled the fug with a genial hum as the masses gathered, jostled, and fought for places at the bar. Half an hour of this, two rounds of drinks on, and the barriers were down, lawyers normally at daggers-drawn with their arms round each others' shoulders slurring exchanges of admiration and goodwill.

The 'guests' are in attendance on sufferance only. After all, no one actually *likes* a banker, or an accountant or a messenger-at arms or an insurance agent even though they have their uses. The Building Society chappie was in a different category, however, since a lawyer's horn of plenty would look pretty empty without the fees associated with property deals which Building Society money, or the lack of it, did much to regulate. Having said this, wee Bert Squeeres was as much of a pain in the neck as Braynes, Cotterill and Stones, though infinitely more useful. Tonight, it had strained our lawyers' good manners to breaking point just to avoid a situation in which the guests were bundled together at a table on their own, out of the way of the gathering proper.

At quarter to eight, everyone had taken in just enough booze to feel good. Then it was that the kilted, bearded Hotelier announced to the company that 'DINNER IS SERVED'.

Duncan, rehearsing his speech whilst at the same time talking to all and sundry, held his head up high and mustered as much dignity as his damaged countenance allowed. Dinner announced, and not looking where he was going, Duncan had tripped over the hotelier's labrador as the beast shambled through the forest of legs, and became up-ended on the only square footage of vacant parquetry in the hotel. Poor Duncan struggled to his feet, his top denture shattered and his face bloodied. Feeling no pain, his first thought was that the swelling of his left cheek, courtesy of Miss Bottoms, could now happily be attributed to his fall. He looked real bonny with no top set and with brownish red stains smudging his face. Nonetheless, he set himself in the crocodile line-up with the rest of the 'Top Table', and awaited with the other dignitaries the summons to enter.

All others seated in the banqueting hall, the Beard announced further – 'Pray be upstanding for your Top Table.'

All upstood, swayed, and laboriously applauded the shamble of weirdos as they entered, in this order:-

Sheriff Clapp
Mr Duncan Smile
Chief Constable Thrashman
Vice-Dean of Faculty, Quintin Tidd
Sheriff Principal, StJohn Shoelace
Dean of Faculty, Benjamin Doon
Mr Jacob Goldnuckle, M.P.
Lord Fraytrouser
Provost Smirk
Sheriff Marbles, and
Adam Braces, Dinner Organiser.

'All be seated,' boomed the Beard, and the Dean of Faculty, left on his feet, said Grace.

This formality seen to, hands stretched out in unison across the tablecloths like seaweed in an eddy, clutched bottles, swept back, again in unison, filled glasses, and commenced to quench and devour.

This went on unabated amidst guffaw-peppered hubbub for all of two hours as nine courses came and went in a crescendo of plates, cutlery, glass and associated clatter. The only noteworthy occurrence was when a guest of Messrs J. & G. Crudd fell off his chair and was carried out unconscious covered in his own vomit shouting subconsciously the kind of obscenities normally heard only on BBC 2. The mess cleared, or nearly cleared (thank God that crew were at the far end of the dining-room), the Dean welcomed hosts and guests in the most pedantic and embarrassing fashion. Grovelling to Lords, Sheriffs, Bishops, Provosts, Members of Parliament and their like is always expected at such gatherings, and no matter how adept the Chairman in his attempt to avoid clichés, grovelling is still grovelling, and it always comes over precisely like insincere crap – because that's precisely what it is even if some of the guests are held in some warmth.

Dean Ben Doon introduced the first speaker – eventually – and Chief Constable Thrashman rose to his feet, eyes glazed, and cheeks roseate.

'Mister Dean, Lord Fraytrouser, Mr Goldnuckle, Sheriffs, Mister Provost, Honoured Guests, Gentlemen......'

At this stage, the public address system broke down, and the company chatted among itself during what was expected to be a temporary lull. Thrashman didn't stop, but no one tried all that hard to listen to the speaker's continuing efforts to be heard. Duncan was able to tell the others the following Monday that they'd missed nothing.

When Thrashman finally sat down, half-hearted applause worked its way slowly from the Top Table to the far corners as each table in succession twigged to the fact that the Chief had stopped talking. One drunk from the far corner – probably an Estate Agent – got to his feet excitedly, clapping extremely heartily, and shouting 'MORE'. He got a predictable mixed reception.

Lord Fraytrouser, that most distinguished High Court Judge, spoke for thirty-five minutes, periodically collapsing with laughter at his own jokes – which not even the few persons who heard them could understand.

They actually got to hear the last few moments of His Lordship's oration as the public address system crackled into fresh life following a bit of wire-twiddling by the perspiring Beard, now stripped to kilt and khaki vest, and wringing with acrid sweat.

'Curse that bloody microphone,' snarled Ray, as Fraytrouser's sonorous drone boomed out once again. 'Why can't these buggers shut up while we're trying to enjoy ourselves?' Bert Squeeres smiled at the comment, just as guests are meant to.

Two Speakers to go. Our Member of Parliament, and the toothless Duncan. God help us!

Duly introduced with a sickly dose of sugary platitudes, up stood Jacob Goldnuckle, M.P. His fruity accent was pure unashamed imported mid European Jewish. Shoulders hunched, and arms bent like clock hands set at ten to two, Jacob's pudgy extremities gesticulated as only such a person can. Mr Goldnuckle didn't require a Star of David stamped on his forehead to vouch for his ancestry.

Jacob came over oily and smooth. The P.A. was at its Sabbath best as if made in Tel Aviv for Israelites, with only the occasional piercing whistle to frighten the comatose throng to a few seconds of semi-silence.

'Enough already, I should be so lucky,' Jacob concluded, 'to be in such a distinguished company. Who am I,' he shrugged, 'Who am I, I ask mineself, to be addressing a legal peoples except as I am a law-abiding citizen? Member of Parliament I am, perhaps, for a while. But vot iss mine Membership of Parliament come the election, I ask? Well, I'll tell you, that's vot I'll do. Each five years I have to pass an exam or unemployed I am. God should punish us all so we haff a quinquennial test of competency to earn a living? Would that I verr a lawyer – just to scrape through an examination when young enough to study with joy in my heart – then to live secure forever. I don't ask you should support mine party, gentlemen – just you should vote me another spell of employment. You don't vont your old friend Jacob just another unemployment statistic?

'Thank you for your sumptuous hospitality – your pork tastes better than mine Rabbi had given me to believe! Thank you for your patience and your warmth – vich you may wish to convert into actual support – you vill find mine upturned cap at the doorside as you leave.'

Jacob winked, shrugged yet again, and sat down.

Mr Goldnuckle did, in fact, receive sympathetic applause apposite to his closing remarks. Another of Messrs Crudd's table passed out, and the poker school, which had got under way at the farthest table through the archway was getting boisterous.

Duncan finished the remains of his brandy, so increasing the bloodflow from his facial wounds, wiped most of the blood from his chin with a fouled red hanky, and – with a minimum of introduction – (it is now 11.45 p.m.) – stood up.

He broke into a broad, gummy grin, creating the most amusing effect of the evening thus far, and got off to a bold start amidst drunken impatience.

'Mr Dean, other high-ranking over-paid twits, nonentities, gentlemen and poofs,' he started, swaying noticeably and with a fresh trickle of blood at each side of his mouth. 'You haven't given any of the bloody speakers a proper hearing. You have been abysmally rude to your friggin' guests. I don't care if Thrashman *did* talk a load of piffle. God knows Fraytrouser needs locking up. And who the hell is Goldnuckle to suggest we sit exams to stay in practice!' Duncan thundered the table, and continued, now in full sail –

'Do Goldnuckle's co-directors at his warehouse make *him* sit a test to stay as a director? Do they buggery! Goldnuckle owns 90% of the shares, that's why!'

All ears and eyes became riveted on Duncan. Even the card-sharpers called an interval.

'I'm telling you lot straight,' Duncan slurred on. 'You're a collection of bloody hypocrites. You dress up like gentlemen and think that you *are* gentlemen. I tell you – *I* can count the gentlemen here on the fingers of one hand!'

Duncan held aloft five bitten fingers. Catching the sight of Revd Father O'Squish just as the man of the cloth downed a good half tumbler of whisky in a solitary gulp, Duncan theatrically lowered one bitten finger, and glowered at the Reverend to the latter's manifest disquiet.

'In *less* than one hand, I say! All the dinner suits in the world can't disguise what *you* lot are – you're a big heap of festering excrement'.

Duncan reached for his re-charged glass, gulped a couple of giant-sized mouthfuls, turned white, and blacked out.

In the process of falling across the table, he pulled the microphone violently from its socket causing an almighty, flashing and resounding explosion – and the whole of the hotel was plunged into total darkness.

The Beard cursed the loss of a fortune in after-hours drinks. The bedlam was deafening as collisions, smashing glasses, pushing, shoving, retching and swearing took command. Someone 'accidentally' broke a chair over Thrashman's head. Dean Doon tried to un-kilt the Beard, and got a cracked jaw for reward. The empty wine-bottle hurled by the only member at Crudd's table who could stand shattered the ornate chandelier, which for its part fragmented over the panic-stricken escapees like confetti.

Ray and Jerry made an instinctive dive to rescue Duncan, dragged him out of the hotel like firemen from a holocaust, and shoved him bodily into a waiting taxi. They watched him departing, struggling, with an inane grin, semi-conscious, and streaming blood down his shirt. Then they staggered up the road together.

'That's more like the thing!' said Ray enthusiastically.

'True,' came Jerry's tired response as he lit a fag with difficulty – 'Best Dinner we've had for years.'

THE BEGINNING

'Dearly beloved, we are gathered here today to join this man – oops, sorry – to celebrate the long and useful life of our late friend Henry Elmer Jeremiah Chancer, affectionately known as "the Hedge", or was it "the Fence", because he spent a lot of time in court defending persons suspected of resetting stolen goods.'

Revd. Petty's feeble attempt at levity fell flat on the mourners at the crematorium. The clergyman clearly didn't know that the deceased, though a competent enough lawyer, was not renowned for any courtroom skills, and had stopped going near any courtroom at all following on a string of humiliating defeats.

'We extend our sympathy to Mr Chancer's family and friends and ask for the blessing of Almighty God on all of them, and on all of you who share their loss……'

Twenty minutes later, the traditional readings and prayers said, the service ended with that well-known hymn 'The day thou gavest Lord is ended', and then the procession filed out into the sunshine en route for the Savaloy Hotel, at which refreshments were to be provided for all interested.

The late Mr Chancer's surviving partners had decided to skip the Savaloy. They had more pressing matters in mind. Like, in what proportions were they to carve up the deceased's share of partnership profits! Eagerness to see this resolved saw Duncan Smile, Jerome Quid and Raymond Squeeze drive straight back to the office at Chancer Chambers.

Duncan's room was its usual shambles, only there had been cleared enough space on his desk to accommodate a large bottle of champagne and three glasses.

'Firstly,' smirked Duncan 'we must drink to the health of the deceased.'

With this announcement made, Duncan eased the cork out of the bottle and ceremoniously poured three glasses of bubbly. Three eager hands stretched out, all stood, and each murmured something different before pouring the effervescent fluid down enthusiastic throats.

Duncan re-loaded the glasses, then with a wide grin which caused his upper set to all but fall out, boomed

'TO US!'

The right note now struck, the trio thought to get down to the business of the hour. But the earlier sunshine had left the sky, and dark storm-clouds enshrouded the town. Henry Chancer's surviving partners began to feel uneasy as the wind whipped up, the room darkened and fierce gusts of rain battered the windows to the south-west.

The three looked querulously at each other.

'Do you think old Henry's angry with us for doing this too quickly?' thought Jerry aloud.

'Bollocks!' snapped Ray, 'Let's get on with it!'

'All right then,' agreed Duncan, 'perhaps we should get on with it, as Ray has invited so eloquently. Can we take it that I will chair the meeting?'

Seeing no reason to object Jerry and Ray nodded agreement.

'Shall we take minutes?' enquired Duncan.

'As long as you don't take bloody hours you can suit yourself. I'm due on the first tee at five o'clock, if the rain clears that is,' Ray responded impatiently.

'That gives us three hours,' mused Duncan.

'I'd have reckoned three minutes to be long enough,' yawned Jerry. 'We are talking about carving up the old man's thirty per cent. I propose we take ten per cent each.'

'I second the motion,' joined Ray.

'Just a minute,' growled Duncan. 'I am now the Senior Partner, and my seniority carries with it responsibilities which require their just reward.'

'Just reward your arse,' spat Ray. 'Your elevated position as SENIOR partner,' he sneered, 'is a fat lot of good to the firm between 8.30 a.m. and 10.30 a.m. when you aren't here, and it's no good at all when you arrive hung-over and leave for the day shortly afterwards. If you want your seniority respected in cash, you'll need to put in some time at your desk for a change. In fact, I withdraw my support for Mr Quid's motion and propose that you take a cut!'

Duncan's face, even his nose, turned white, and he fumbled in his desk drawer for a bottle of pills, opened the child-proof lid with difficulty, removed and swallowed two pills with the dregs of his champagne and dropped the rest on the floor.

'I am not a well man,' he quivered. 'My doctor says I am suffering from executive syndrome and that I must ration my exposure to stress. But he has agreed with me that I can do more useful and productive work in an hour than some people can do in a whole day.'

Duncan then nervously raised his eyes to assess his partners' reaction to his words.

Jerry and Ray sat in silence for a few moments, and then Ray enquired sarcastically, 'Did your doctor not suggest that retirement would be a preferred option for someone with such, eh, indifferent health?'

Duncan had a glazed look in his eyes.

'If only I could retire,' he said quietly at last, 'but I have so much to give the community, specially now that Henry has gone, God bless him.'

'We'll be getting the tears next,' said Ray nudging Jerry.

Jerry, who had been mainly a listener, decided it was his turn.

'Look here, boys,' he ventured, 'this has been a hard time for all of us. Old Henry's death has us all in shock to an extent. This is, or should be, a new beginning for us all. I would like us three to start again, as it were, with shared responsibility and shared profits and losses – each as equals of the other. None of us will starve with thirty three and a third per cent each, and maybe the goodwill to each other of equal sharing will bring out the best of our efforts and co-operation. Maybe we should open that other bottle of champagne – one of those you hid in your bookcase for taking home, Duncan – and toast our new and friendlier relationships. What do you think?'

Shamefaced, Duncan limped over to the bookcase and removed a second bottle. Easing off its cork – this time with a real 'Pop' – Duncan enquired, 'How did you bastards know about the second bottle?'

'We know about the other four also,' replied Jerry. 'The invoice for six made out to the firm, arrived with the morning mail that you're never here to see.'

Duncan poured three glasses and smiled sheepishly. Each was downed with a unanimous toast 'Equal Partners'.

Largely unseen, the rain had eased off and there were gaps in the clouds. As the last of the second bottle was finished, the sun broke through and Duncan's dingy room was bathed in light.

'You'll make your golf game in tons of time' smirked Jerry, as they left Chancer Chambers together. As usual, of course, Ray set off for his 'Royal' course having carefully omitted to take his wallet with him. This new beginning at Chancers wouldn't change that habit of a lifetime.

DUNCAN'S MORNING

'You fine specimen of manhood – strong masculine features, Gregory Peck nose, aristocratic jaw-line, Kirk Douglas dimple – sheer geometric perfection…..'

So audibly did Duncan address his soap splashed shaving-mirror that Doreen switched off her leg-razor to catch her beloved's finale –

'Just to see you each morning is reason enough to waken. Have a nice day.'

Duncan always started the day with a prayer of thanksgiving for his good looks and fortune, and adoringly caressed his face with the same months' old disposable blade, cursing the transience of its sharpness as he applied toilet tissue to the worst of his self-inflicteds.

'What was that you said?' enquired Doreen, as she re-engaged her own depilatory device.

'I can't hear what you're saying with that thing on,' was Duncan's disinterested response.

Doreen switched off again, yanking out with a yell a thick longish hair by its root.

'Why don't you let the bloody things grow, woman? The way you're going your legs will be like doormats. At least with another couple of centimetres you'll be able to keep your stockings up without suspenders.'

Duncan had a thing about stockings, and it mattered nothing to him about the legs within.

'That's right, Doreen, grow a decent thatch and let's see these stockings stay up by themselves!'

Doreen burst into tears and trembled downstairs in her equally burst dressing gown. She could take the abuse about her stubbly legs, but there was no way in which she could have faced her husband's arrival in the dining room without having his hot breakfast awaiting his pompous arrival.

As Duncan crossed the dining room threshold, Doreen tonged rashers of bacon and two fried eggs from the sideboard servery on to a pre-heated plate and deferentially laid the steaming offering before her master, at the same time flicking open a crisp linen napkin and draping it across his badly stained trousers.

'No mushrooms, Doreen?' enquired her husband. 'Or kidneys?'

'I'm afraid not dear – you had the last of both with your toast at bed-time last night, don't you remember?'

Duncan belched with remembrance and set about his breakfast – without a murmur of appreciation. After his third cup of percolated coffee, and a preliminary glance at the tabloids, Duncan took the *Sun* upstairs to the bathroom in order at least partially to evacuate his digestive intake of the last twelve hours. Being a working day, he had to get a move on. A glance at his watch told him it was 11.20 a.m. 'No time for elevenses,' he called to Doreen as he slammed out the front door. 'Duty calls!'

Ten minutes later, Duncan slumped into his office chair, phoned Miss Bottoms for a coffee, then summoned Darkie his Secretary and gave the poor soul his wife's shopping list and less than half the money necessary to pay for it.

Whilst sucking his coffee audibly through his cracked dentures, Duncan fumbled in the bottom drawer of his desk and drew out a fifteen year old Motor Show Magazine and drooled over the fancy machines for which he had then yearned, but couldn't at that time, raise the fifteen hundred quid price.

'Those were the days,' he muttered as Jerry strolled into his reverie without knocking.

'So you're here at last,' sneered Jerry. 'What's today's story about your 11.30 arrival? Have you any idea how much work has already been done by those whom you continue to classify as your juniors?'

Slamming a fat file on top of his magazine, Duncan rose to his feet angrily and spat out his customary response –

'Now look here, Quid. You and Squeeze may *think* you are working just by being here. But there's a lot more to legal practice than putting in the hours. Where would you be today if it weren't for me, channelling a fortune in clients through those doors so that you can feel worthwhile?

I'll tell you where I have been this morning. I have been out earning the firm's goodwill by being with the right people in the right places....'

Jerry cut him off, 'Spare me the crap, Mr Smile – being in bed with Doreen until mid-morning might be your idea of hard work – it must certainly be tough going for Doreen – but the only goodwill involved is that you can't do the Firm much damage while you're not here.'

Duncan lunged forward for his pill bottle, and washed down a couple of tranquillisers with a cold coffee chaser, turned red and yelled 'Get out of here, you swine!' and slumped back in his chair, the roseate colour draining out of his cheeks and his upper set clicking loose on to its lower companions.

'The Watsons are in the waiting-room for you if you have a minute,' grimaced Jerry as he made for the door.

'Mr Quid,' gasped Duncan. 'Jerry, I mean…. Be a good chap and see the Watsons for me. These are the kind of persons I urge to see such as yourself who are more on their wavelength.'

'Mr Watson,' replied Jerry, 'is more on *your* wavelength, Duncan. He is a rat catcher and I suggest, not only that *you* should see him, but that you don't do as you did with that Wine Merchant chappie you saw on Friday afternoon.'

'What do you mean?'

'I mean don't spend hours with Mr Watson asking to sample his produce!'

OGLES AND THE TURDS

It's distinctly unusual for Messrs Chancer's Waiting Room to fill up much earlier than ten o'clock. Either clients are themselves slow to stir themselves into alertness or else they share the belief, not altogether unjustified, that lawyers are slow off the mark – physically, mentally or both. One such unusual day found six persons seated before 9.15 a.m. in cold uncharitable surroundings, two shaking, two coughing and the others pained-looking as if at the doctor's. The early start to this day's agonies was but the first of a number of unusual events to occur before closing time was to bring its relief.

As the six shuffled their feet on the threadbare carpet to keep warm, Jerry was in his room lighting a relaxing fag and recovering from opening the morning's mail. Raymond was stuck in a traffic jam picking bacon out his teeth with a pin. Duncan was tucked up in bed dreaming that he had been locked in a wine cellar. Of the patient six, Mr and Mrs Tommy Ogles were waiting on Jerry, and the other four – a well-dressed middle aged couple with two punk teenagers of indeterminate sex – were waiting for Duncan. Theirs would be the patience most sorely stretched.

Tommy Ogles was scanning undies adverts in a 1964 Harpers & Queen when Jerry stuck his head round the door and invited the couple to 'walk this way'. When the Ogles pair were comfy across Jerry's desk (not literally) he lit another fag having had his offer of nicotinic refreshment waved aside by his clients.

'We are from the Brethren Hall, Mr Quid, and we don't smoke.'

'Very commendable,' smiled Jerry, refraining from asking what they did instead.

'Cold morning, Mr Quid,' offered Mr Ogles.

'Indeed it is, sir. But I hope you are comfortable here. In what way can I be of help?'

'You tell him, Maisie,' said Tommy gloomily, not raising his eyes from his knees.

'Well, it's like this, Mr Quid. Mr Ogles was out walking to the newsagents for his evening paper when a police van stopped and asked him to go to the station. Mr Ogles asked what it was about, but they said he'd be told when he got to the station. When he got there, a constable said that Mr Ogles was being charged with indecent exposure in the Ladies' Toilets at the Cross. And he's never been to the Ladies Toilets, have you, Tommy?'

'No Maisie,' whispered the gent, eyes still lowered.

'Who made the complaint to the police, Mrs Ogles?' Jerry decided that there was no point, at this stage anyway, in asking anything directly of the lady's husband.

'Apparently, two women in the toilets said that Mr Ogles *staggered* into the conveniences and, er, opened his coat.'

'Maybe your husband went into the 'Ladies' by accident, thinking it was the 'Gents' – and, if he was in a hurry it would be quite natural for him to unbutton his coat immediately he was off the pavement?'

'I suggested to my husband that it was probably that way, but apparently the women weren't convinced that there was any accident. They told the police that his 'posture', I think they called it, was not consistent with any accident. That's what they said, wasn't it, Tommy?'

'Yes, Maisie, something like that.'

Mr Ogles top lip was heavy with beads of nervous sweat, which he wiped aside with the back of his hand without raising his eyes.

'The women,' continued Mrs Ogles, 'said they could identify him by his pink underpants with a flower motif at the waistband. Right enough, Mr Quid, that's what he was wearing, but surely they're ten a penny, and it could have been anyone wearing the same garment?'

'Quite so, Mrs Ogles,' replied Jerry, swallowing uneasily in shock. 'Any M and S Store, I'd think – did the women identify your husband in any other way? Has he attended an identity parade with all the men wearing the same knickers – eh, underpants, I mean?'

'Yes and no, Mr Quid. My husband did attend an identity parade, but the police refused to make them all wear the same pants. In fact Mr Ogles was wearing his lilac pants at the parade, but the two bitches still picked him out – they said they recognised the fiery boil on his neck.'

Jerry looked up from his notepad and though Mr Ogles' head was still lowered, the plaster on his swollen neck stood out, barely covering the roseate beacon which overflowed it, glowing cheerily.

'I think Mr Qgles may have a wee problem here, Madam.'

'Not really, Mr Quid, he's getting it lanced this afternoon.'

'Not the boil, Mrs Ogles – the charge against your husband. It looks as if there's some substance in it, as well as in the boil.'

'Could you not say he's insane, Mr Quid?'

'Is he?'

'Not a mile off it, if you ask me – you should have seen the women!!'

'Well, Mrs Ogles, my advice is that your husband should plead 'Guilty' leaving it for my court Assistant to explain that it was an unfortunate accident and that positively no offence to the ladies was intended. Why, the Court appearance could be over in a flash.'

'Does that mean I've got to do it again in court?' wakened Mr Ogles.

'Not at all, sir – just make sure that when you are served with a summons it's handed in here straightaway.'

'Does that mean that my husband will get approbation?' re-entered the wife.

'Not exactly, Mrs Ogles, though your husband may have to see a Social Worker – but that's all for the future. Not to worry for the moment.'

'Can I have a drink now Maisie?' the accused asked his wife.

'Not till you get home,' frowned the lady. Turning to Jerry, she explained 'I let my husband have some tonic wine occasionally for his nerves. The Oversight at the Hall said that it would be all right.'

'Oh I *am* glad, Mrs Ogles. I take the occasional glass of tonic wine myself – does wonders for the system,' smiled the lawyer as he rose and beckoned the couple to the door marked 'Exit' past Duncan's still expectant quartette.

Duncan was awake by this time; not that it was easy to tell the difference. Sitting on the bed with reddened eyelids still stuck to his upper cheek, he scratched his white torso through his overnight string vest and tried to stir some life into his body by wriggling his toes. He had read in some angling magazine that this prevented cramp and aided circulation whilst waiting on some riverbank for a bite.

Half an hour later, and after a fulsome breakfast and a brace of hearty belches, Duncan wedged himself into his Granada and drove ponderously the five hundred yards to the office carpark, then shambled on foot the remaining hundred yards to the office itself, sighing wearily all the way.

Quarter of an hour later, at goodness knows when, Mr Duncan Smile walked into the waiting room and asked the four Franklins to follow him along the dismal corridor to his room.

The two punks parked their gum politely inside copies of *Good Housekeeping*, and followed their parents, sniggering.

Waving the parents to the two more comfortable old seats of the five strewn about his 'chambers' Duncan apologised sickenly for keeping the Franklins waiting, explaining that, between Church meetings and late work hours and his indolent wife's delays over breakfast – and a few other irrelevancies – his clients were, by implication damn lucky to see him at all, delays or no delays. The two punks nudged and grinned at each other as Duncan rambled on, whilst Reg and Dorothy Franklin just looked bored

Eventually Duncan, who had been standing at the window during his monologue, slumped into his big plastic chair, making a rude noise in the process, much to the mirth of the young ones.

'Damn plastic cushions,' muttered Duncan, 'Make a hellavu noise.' The lawyer then flicked something solid out of his left ear, donned his executive NHS half-glasses and peered over them quizzically.

'Yes?' he enquired. 'I'm a busy man – what are you doing here?'

'Waiting mostly,' sniggered Samantha Franklin, kicking her brother sharply under the table.

'Shut-up Sam,' snapped her mother. 'Reg and I want to buy our council house, Mr Smile, and you've come highly recommended by the children's' gym mistress.'

Duncan coughed dryly, and removed his glasses to wipe away the gathering steam as he conjured up a mental picture of Miss Glandles.

'Very nice, Mrs Franklin. I'm delighted to help any friend of Vandra

Glandles. All you need to do is to tell the District Council Offices that I'm your man, and they'll know to send the relevant papers to my good self.'

'Is that all that's to it?' enquired Mr Franklin.

'Indeed it is, sir,' smiled Duncan whilst fumbling uneasily for the pill bottle in the burst lining of his jacket pocket.

'Even when we've no money?' added Mrs Franklin.

'No money!' thundered Duncan. 'Bloody hell, woman, you can't buy a book of matches without money – how the hell do you expect to buy a house? What do you earn, Mr Franklin?'

'I'm unemployed, sir – but I thought you advertised 100% loans available – it says that you lawyers do this.'

'Only if you have the bloody income to repay the mortgage matey!'

'Would Duane's income help?'

'What on earth is duane?' gulped Duncan.

'I am!' the Mohican boy (it turns out) spoke for the first time, adjusting the gilt pin in his nose.

'Duane is a bass guitarist, Mr Smile,' explained Mr Franklin. 'He earns about £3,000 a week.'

'*Earns*! There's a laugh – sorry, that's unforgivable of me, Duane. What group do you play with?'

'The Turds,' replied the lad.

'Very appropriate!' rejoined Duncan, then continued 'but why don't you just buy your parents the house with your loose change, sonny?'

'I don't think I like your attitude, old man,' spat Duane.

'Old man, is it, you filthy little creep. I'm not going to sit here listening to your insults.'

'Then stand up, fatty and I'll tell you more......'

'Now then, Duane,' chastised his mother. 'It's just that you and Mr Smile have wee musical differences – it's quite natural that an older man like Mr Smile may prefer older music. He still wants to help us all don't you, Mr Smile?'

Duncan thought of Vandra Glandles once again, smiled, and replied, 'Of course, I do, Mrs Franklin. I'll be delighted to fix you up with the purchase *and* a mortgage. And I'm sure that your highly talented son will gladly act as guarantor from his well-deserved earnings.'

Oddly, this seemed to satisfy everyone, notes were duly taken, and Duncan reiterated the pleasure it was going to be for him to do business with Vandra's protégés. As the good lawyer walked the four back along the corridor, he put his hand on Samantha's lacquered green and yellow hair, and enquired, 'And what do you do for a living, young lady?'

'I'm a law student, Mr Smile, and Miss Glandles says she's going to speak to you about getting a job here when I've graduated.'

'By jove, Miss Glandles is most considerate, remembering about me so much! We'll have to see about this once you have your degree. My very best wishes to you with your studies,' he lied.

Once the Franklins had left, Duncan sucked air sharply through his broken dentures and muttered something unmentionable.

At 9.30, or maybe later, Ray had arrived, shut himself into his room and by noon had put in a solid session of routine conveyancing work unlikely to spark the reader's interest. Feeling a glow of accomplishment from such a rare burst of effort, he stood up and stretched himself, took in the damp and unexciting scene on the deserted pavements outside, slumped back into his chair, rested his head on its greasy back, and fell asleep. He was awakened at half past one by his phone. It was his wife Marjory to say that his lunch was burnt to a cinder. Doubting whether this would make any difference to its enjoyment, Ray picked up his coat from the floor and grouched his way downstairs, thence to the carpark, and didn't return that day.

Duncan's afternoon was taken up blethering with four commercial travellers in succession, each of whom ended up with nothing but a confused expression and a sore head. But each of them had received warmth and shelter from the rain, and gave Duncan some 'pressure' to moan about when lingering awhile with the firm's cashier before going home for his gourmet mince.

Jerry stopped smoking at lunchtime so that he could truthfully complete a non-smoker's life insurance proposal at 3 p.m. but had lapsed accidentally whilst the Insurance Agent was still in his room, and had to initial the alteration on the proposal form. Thereafter, he went to his local surgery for the associated 'medical' and gave his doctor a good laugh as he bared his skeleton for examination.

The acceptance note that subsequently arrived from the insurance company gave Jerry some surprised pleasure, and he lit a fag to celebrate.

COMPLAINT

Ray and Jerry poured over the morning mail, slashing envelope after envelope and scanning the contents of each with a mixture of mirth and alarm, sober interest and downright panic. Halfway through the daily chore, both lawyers simultaneously held aloft a piece of paper in the mode of Neville Chamberlain in 1939.

'You know how sometimes it's difficult keeping your breakfast down!' quipped Ray rhetorically, wearing a big grin atop a half-shaven chin to whose bristles some dried-up egg adhered colourfully.

'Don't talk to me about keeping your breakfast down!' snapped Jerry in response, somewhat less gleeful of expression.

'What does yours say?' enquired Ray, becoming serious.

'You first, laughing boy' Jerry replied, not removing his eyes from the letter in his hand.

Ray's grin reappeared. 'Oh, it's just Mrs Gow. She wants to change her will for the hundredth time. Apparently her neighbour has cut the hedge between their grotty houses a couple of inches too low, so the fifty pound legacy which had been left to 'her dearest friend' Jessie Hyslop is to be cancelled forthwith!'

'Big deal,' frowned Jerry.

'Your turn,' smiled Ray.

'Oh, it's nothing important. Just about a complaint to the Law Society by Sprocket Engineering that Mr Smile has dropped them in the fertiliser – here, look!!'

Ray ignored the short letter addressed to the firm by the secretary of the Law Society – he'd seen the like before – and concentrated his gaze on the six foolscap pages of close typescript to which it was attached. These pages set out the grounds of complaint at length, on which the brief Law Society missive politely invited comments 'at your early convenience'.

'It'll never be convenient to reply to this catalogue of accusations, mate. And God knows what mess Duncan will make of his efforts to do so. The cardinal rule is to say nothing, and if nothing won't do, the next rule is to say as little as possible. Heaven help us, that bastard Smile will dictate a veritable book of replies, packed full of inaccuracies, inconsistencies, admissions, contradictions – enough to hang the lot of us. The only consolation is that he's so bloody ungrammatical and his typist is so bloody useless that no one will be able to make any sense of what he says, and may even rightly assume that the man has lost his marbles. Then he'll claim that he wrote it whilst gravely ill, deny having meant the bits that damn us, blame us, his indolent partners, for having pushed him over the top, come out the clean potato and get us two struck off!!'

Quite a mouthful from Ray so early in the day, his face becoming roseate and twisted in anger.

'Maybe *we* should reply?' offered Jerry.

'No, *I* will reply' soured Ray, leaving his unopened mail and heading for his room. 'No time like the present.'

At 4.30 p.m. a huge bundle of typed letters on his desk ready for signing, Ray read aloud to Jerry the reply of which he had spoken some eight hours earlier –

'Dear Mr Secretary,
Sprocket Engineering – Complaint
We thank you for drawing to our attention that Messrs Sprocket Engineering have submitted a complaint about the quality of legal services received by that company in consultation with one of our partners, Mr Duncan Smile. It is owing to Mr Smile's absence through illness that the writer is responding as requested by you.

Messrs Sprocket seem to believe that a complaint becomes justified by the sheer volume of the words employed to express it, but, for the life of us, we cannot see the relevancy of the complaint or any accountability on our part for the supposed losses which Messrs Sprocket allege. It seems to have become popular for clients to complain about their solicitors when they don't, or can't, get all that they want, and this seems to be a rather typical example, a view which we invite you to share with us.

You may assure Messrs Sprocket that any remaining doubts or queries will receive our usual helpful and understanding attention should they

get in touch with us. And we apologise on their behalf for the unnecessary trouble to which they have put you.
  With the writer's kindest regards,
  Yours sincerely
  Raymond Squeeze'

'That should do the trick, Jerome – apologise for the client not for yourself. The client is always wrong in such circumstances. Say nothing to Mr Smile about this. I'll deal with him if there's any backfire. Mark my words, I WILL!!'

Peculiarly, there was no backfire.

Three months later, and with Ray's file on the matter marked 'Closed' on the basis of a friendly Law Society letter to the effect that the complaint had been withdrawn, the wicked Mr Squeeze obliterated the date of the original complaint and left it among Duncan's mail on a wet Monday, with a scribbled memo requiring that Duncan must show his intended observations in response before attempting any reply.

Duncan's draft reply, two days later, read as follows, exactly as typed, word for bleeding word –

'Dear Mr Secretary
Sprocket Engineering Claim V our Firm
I, Duncan Smile, Senior partner of this firm, am honoured to have received your letter (undated) enclosing a claim by Sprocket Engineering (also undated) and feel obligated to retort in this manner, following numerically the numbered paragraphs of the Sprocket complaint to coincide with the numbered paragraphs hereof, viz:-

1. Yes, I am indeed Senior Partner of Henry Chancer & Co Solicitors, and yes I was consulted on behalf of Sprocket Engineering by their Mr Spanner (Director) and Mr Toolie (Secretary). My diary clearly evidences meetings between me and these gentlemen on four occasions in April of this year. I noted their instructions with my usual meticulous attention to detail and passed them to my secretary for typing. Unfortunately,

she had to go into hospital to have her appendix removed, and no one could find my notes prior to a fifth meeting in May, so I had to tell Messrs Spanner and Toolie that *per incuriam* the work instructed, through no fault of my own, had not been commenced, but would be put in hand with some immediacy on my secretary's return to business. In the event, rather than have her appendix removed, it transpired that my secretary was some eight months pregnant (you couldn't have told) was delivered prematurely of male triplets and hasn't been back at work since. Happily mother and children are doing well. My notes never turned up, which I told Messrs Sprocket explicitly through the good offices of Mr Toolie's wife when I met her one evening in the off-licence, and that I would need to be re-instructed on behalf of the company.

2. Mr Toolie's wife did not, apparently, relay the message to her husband who, with the directors of Sprocket, mistakenly believed (thanks to Mrs Toolie's neglect) that I had taken action on their original instructions. I blame Mrs Toolie unreservedly for the misunderstanding on the part of the Sprocket directors who, for their part, were singularly remiss in having failed to enquire the progress of their business of which there had been none for the reasons explained.

3. I am an extremely busy solicitor, who does not, regrettably, enjoy good health. I rely on clients to take an active interest in all items of business committed to my charge. It's their business, after all, not mine. How else can I remember every trifling detail of the scores of instructions which pour on to my desk, rather than on to the desks of my junior partners. Mark you, it's maybe not their fault that I am the one held in highest esteem. All too often, however, my breakdowns of health and concentration arise because I am victim of my own renown at dealing with the highest standards of professional competence. There must be a number of Senior Partners like me who will know what I am talking about.

4. When I was an apprentice in Dundee, I was always taught to admit my mistakes – not to look for excuses. I admit that I was overworked at the relevant times. I admit that my doctor had told me to double

my daily Valium intake because of excessive pressures on me. I admit that Sprockets instructed me after a fashion, but not in writing and not with adequate clarity for my understanding given the state of my health. I admit the possibility, no more than this, mind, that Sprockets *may* feel me responsible for the loss of which they write – but, I ask you, £100,000 just because I missed out on the matter so that the take-over of their company fell through. Their company wasn't worth taking over, believe me. No wonder they are suffering from sour grapes. Sprockets may have missed out on making a lot of money, but look how the intending take-over company has been saved the injustice of paying through the nose for a dud concern. I feel almost public-spirited and as if I have been an inert instrument of justice. I make no apology in that fairness has prevailed. Having said this, I have properly written to the Indemnity Company intimating that a claim has been received, but have confidently predicted that the claim, if resisted, will come to nought if considerations of natural justice prevail – and I expect that you, Sir, will not find it difficult to appreciate my position.

This letter, as ever, conveys my best regards to your goodladywife and yourself. See you at the Society's wine tasting on 17th when we can get out of our mouths once and for all the bad taste to which such trouble-some circumstances can give rise.

Yours most sincerely.'

'Bloody Hell! He's done it again' gritted Ray to Jerry, tearing up the draft into small pieces. 'Better tell him the truth?'

Ray and Jerry barged into Duncan's room. He had his top denture out picking at slivers of meat with his pencil. On having heard what Ray had to say, Duncan replaced his denture and smiled.

'You don't actually think I'd have sent the letter, do you? That new secretary of mine got my dictation all wrong and created what seems to be quite the wrong impression'.

'THE WRONG IMPRESSION – too bloody true, mate,' his partners chorused.

BEENIE GRONNIX

'That's Mrs Beenie Gronnix in to see you, Mr Quid,' announced Mrs Mulcaster by intercom.

'*The* Beenie Gronnix?' joked Jerry, smiling to himself.

'Just a moment and I'll find out, Mr Quid,' came the reply.

'*Don't*!!' yelled Jerry. But his phone was dead. Half a minute later, Mrs Mulcaster belled through again.

'Mr Quid, Mrs Gronnix says she didn't realise you *had* more than one client called Beenie Gronnix, but she thinks she's the most important Mrs Gronnix who wants to see you this afternoon. And, as if to emphasise the point, Mrs Gronnix adds that she's the only person in the waiting room.'

Barely able to contain his irritation at the stupidity of his telephonist, Jerry quietly suggested that Mrs Gronnix should be shown into his office. Jerry had never heard of the woman, and didn't imagine that persons with such names existed outside Spike Milligan's fertile imagination. His door opened wide and a very pregnant and unpretty woman was shown in. Matted hair of indeterminate gingerish colour framed a pudgy face with shining red cheeks and nose, thick black eyebrows like Dennis Healey, two teeth missing from the front of her upper set and a fair copse of curly hair sprouting from her chin. Her greenish tweed coat was necessarily unbuttoned, showing beneath a very much uncoordinated woollen dress, the stains on which were largely swallowed up in garish patterns of gold, blue and brown. A less likely candidate for pregnancy was hard to imagine.

'Come away in, Mrs Gronnix – have a seat' smiled Jerry. The thought that she should need *both* seats rose and subsided unspoken.

'*Miss* Gronnix,' came the guttural reply.

'Of course, *Miss* Gronnix,' agreed Jerry, wishing to put the lady at her ease, but uneasy himself about the swell of the maiden's abdomen and how soon it may deflate in childbirth. 'What may I do to help?'

'Well, a friend of mine has got a problem.'

'Your friend has got a problem?' Jerry instantaneously regretted his emphasis, but Beenie, apparently, couldn't muster the intelligence to take offence.

'Yes, sir. My friend Sybil McBrick has got herself into the club, and the man involved wants nothing to do with her.'

'Poor Mrs McBrick,' mused Jerry aloud.

'*Miss* McBrick, sir'.

'Oh dear, what a pity. I take it Miss McBrick knows who the father is, and his whereabouts.'

'Oh yes, sir, and he was always thereabouts – sometimes four times a week.'

'Ah ha,' muttered Jerry, taking indecipherable pencil notes on a pad. 'And what does your friend want to do? I mean, she has asked you to call and see me. Is it advice she wants – indeed what kind of advice does she want?'

'I don't know, Mr Quid, she didn't tell me.'

Jerry realised he had reached the end of the cul-de-sac, and looked for a way back out.

'Now, let's see, Miss Gronnix. Your friend is pregnant. The father of her unborn child called on her four times a week at about the time the child was conceived. He has been told of your friend's condition, and he has upped and offed and left her to carry the can. He was perfectly happy to make her pregnant, but wants nothing to do with the baby – or with Sybil for that matter. And Sybil is torn between openly holding the man responsible for her condition – and the financial consequence of the child's upbringing – or alternatively should she continue on her own, without him and procure all the Social Services and State Security support available?'

Jerry knew, even as he spoke, that Beenie wouldn't have remembered the first part of his address by the time he got to the second part.

'Pardon?' gaped Miss Gronnix.

'Does Sybil want the man back?' simplified Jerry.

'Sybil can't have him back – he's now living with me.'

'WHAT?' exploded Jerry with disbelief.

'Well, remember I said the man was 'with' Sybil four times a week. Well, he was 'with' me four times a week too, and when me and Sybil were having a wee wine together, it all came out, see? We had a big argument, and faced big Bernard with a choice. Her or me like. And big Bernard chose me.'

'And you say Sybil is the one with the problem! Surely both of you have a problem.'

'Not now that big Bernard has made up his mind. You see, Sybil isn't that attractive a person to look at.'

Jerry gulped incredulously. 'So you are happy for yourself, for big Bernard and about your pregnancy.'

'Oh yes, sir. Big Bernard is a lovely man. He bought me all these clothes, so he did. All on the one day. Brought them to me in a big sack, like Santa Claus, and made me try them on there and then.'

'And what about Sybil?'

'She can earn her clothes from someone else from now on. I want you to write a lawyer's letter and tell her to lay off big Bernard from now on or I'll melt her.'

'Perhaps I would need to word my letter in slightly different terms.'

'Any threatening letter will do, Mr Quid. Sybil will know what to expect from me if she comes the bag.'

Jerry believed her.

'Now to conclude Miss Gronnix – you started by saying your friend had a problem – but you haven't said what I can do to help.'

'Yes I have! Her problem is me if she doesn't obey your lawyer's letter – that's all there is to it!'

With this Jerry's phone rang. Mrs Mulcaster announced that 'Mrs Gronnix's fiancée is in the Waiting Room to collect her.'

Relieved by the interruption, Jerry told his client of the gentleman's arrival.

'That'll be big Bernard, sir; I'd better go now – you *will* remember to write?'

Beenie slipped a piece of dirty paper into Jerry's hand, and, as he involuntary contracted from her scaly touch, noticed that there was scratched on the paper the poor Miss McBrick's address.

Showing the lady out, Jerry cast an eye into the waiting room and caught a glimpse of big Bernard – about 5 feet 1 inch tall, sevenish stones and with a very nasty squint.

'Lucky Sybil McBrick,' Jerry mused, as he walked to his window and flung it open.

THE SERMON

At Duncan's Church, St. Artois, Reverend Petty had decided to relieve himself of sermon preparation twice a year by inviting 'Guest Preachers' to occupy his pulpit on a chosen Sunday each May and November. The Provost, the Chief Constable, Firemaster and Rotary President, had all featured in years past, along with a local G.P., dentist, plumber, joiner etc. Reaching the very bottom of his non-alcoholic barrel, the Reverend approached and booked Duncan Smile late August for the coming November's Service. Duncan, as ever, took the invitation as an honour personally extended to his goodself. After all, none of the other local lawyers had his seniority, his style, education, wisdom and delivery. It didn't occur to him that his 'turn' was long overdue and had been postponed and skated around for as long as Revd. Petty could find just about anyone else to fill the spot.

Of course, Duncan was right not to take the invitation lightly. No one should stand up in God's House in a state of unpreparedness. As Duncan himself said:

'There are souls to be won – this might be my only opportunity to stage a spiritual revival, and such an opportunity mustn't be thrown away with careless words.'

So, through much of September, all of October, and into November Duncan assiduously applied himself to preparation for his big day – and to little else, it must be said.

On the morning of the appointed Lord's Day, Duncan got up early at just after half past nine and had a bath. His suit had been pressed by Doreen and was hanging on his wardrobe door. Although all of his lay-predecessors had turned out dressed smartly for their pulpit – elevation, none had gone to town as Duncan planned to do. His 'court' gown was unearthed from the office for an ecclesiastical outing, and he (fool!) even acquired from theatrical costumiers the white dog-collar and black bib – all without a word to Revd. Petty, of course.

His neck obscured by a Rangers Football Club muffler, Duncan walked to church and joined Revd. Petty in the Vestry, excusing the removal of his outer raiment by virtue of November's early frost. At 11 a.m. the final peal of church bells echoed to silence. The organist, one Bill McGuffie, chorded his way through an obscure anthem and the Church Officer led Revd. Petty and Duncan, like three ducks in a pond, into the church. Duncan had removed his coat on to a peg in the passage just outside the church door, and entered the House of God behind the minister who had no idea that Duncan was clerically attired until both had taken adjacent seats in the raised pulpit. Revd. Petty swallowed hard as the anthem concluded, not just because of Duncan's dog collar, but as much on account of the coloured hood draped round the back of his gown – none other that the Rangers scarf itself. Plus a gold chain of Doreen's with a heavy cross dangling in front of his waistcoat. In his outstretched hand, he held the shaft of a silver and ivory handled shepherd's crook which he had withdrawn from inside his cloak whilst ascending the pulpit steps.

Revd. Petty's brain was in full spin as he stuttered the service into motion, all the time itching to scream his disgust that Duncan should profane the holy place by turning out like the traditional idiot-vicar of a stage farce.

Whilst the service was in progress, Duncan was scanning the congregation. Not even the curiosity-ridden addition of most of Chancer's staff could compensate for the absence of a large section of the usual congregation who had decided to give this Sunday's service a miss, on having read the guest 'preacher's' name on the pavement side notice board. That the church was even half full was a tribute to the loyal devotion of those who did turn up – or maybe they had failed to notice, or had forgotten, that this was Mr Smile's day on duty.

At last the fated time arrived when, the Minister's embarrassed introduction over, Duncan rose to his feet, grasped with one hand the left edge of the big Bible on the lectern whilst leaning on the crook with the other, smiled glaiketly to all and sundry, and then began –

'Dearly beloved, we are gathered here today to worship God in spirit and in truth, and by water and blood. I remember the first time I entered the door of this Church. I was but a lad in short trousers. I saw Doreen, now my wife, sitting in the back row over there, in pigtails, with braces in her teeth and her face covered in spots, and at that very point in time I knew, I just knew, that we were meant for each other. Some years later, Doreen and I took our vows of matrimony right there,' pointing with his crook towards the chancel, and drawing copiously from a glass of water 'Each of our children was baptised in that font, indeed in Perrier water free from spot or stain. I celebrated my first communion at that table, in a blue velvet suit from the Co-op and with new gold confirmation cuff links in my shirt. Solomon in all his glory was not so adorned. Nothing but the best for the Lord of Hosts, I always say.

'The memorial services for each of my late, much loved and highly respected parents were conducted within these sacred walls, and for each of whom the crematorium director stoked a completely new fire of purest fuels. This, my friends, is MY Church, and it is right and fitting that I should now occupy the one place, the pulpit, which has hitherto been occupied by others, most of whom have arrived here as usurpers many years after my spiritual roots had been planted in the sanctity of this place. The circle is now complete. For years, I have listened from the pews. Now I am the preacher to whom others must listen. Behold and listen, my flock, because we may never come this way again. Sufficient unto the day, and all that stuff.'

Revd. Petty held his lowered head in his shaking hands, hoping the end had arrived. Duncan, however, stooped and raised again the water glass to his lips and sipped noisily. Revd. Petty bit his lip, winced, and raised his lowered head to the ceiling as if beseeching divine intervention. His prayer went unanswered.

'Now then, the message. My text is from the Parable of the Sower, and I am here to warn you all about the deceitfulness of riches and how these choke the word and maketh it unfruitful. I am probably richer than any of you. I have saved carefully from my youth, have invested skilfully and have put away thousands of pounds into my personal pension fund. I am, to put it bluntly, a very wealthy man. Now, we all know that it's easier for a camel to go through the eye of a needle than for a rich man to enter the Kingdom of God, so it is necessary that we put something away into God's Bank also, or we have eternal damnation staring us in the face, so to speak. That is why I have one or two £10 covenants to Oxfam, War on Want etc so to be let it be known to the Lord that I am a loving, caring Christian person. Not for me spending all of my money on drink or betting. Oh no – that's not for me. God has given me the skill to accumulate a huge fee-income, so it is only right, meet and proper for me to give God his place. He has all my love and adoration – not to mention my gratitude that He has singled me out as someone special in this community. And if He hasn't, in these latter days, given me the best of health, at least has given me the wherewithal to join BUPA and to go private when I am stricken – as is frequently my sad lot.'

At this point, Duncan clutched at his chest dramatically, leaned heavily on his crook, slipped a couple of pills out of a silver engraved phial and washed them down with more water.

'So I urge you, in all Christian charity, to give generously of your substance as I do, and if yours is no more than the widow's mite, which by appearances may well be the case, give it gladly in love. There is no other way. I would love to give more of my substance but I have lent all my uncommitted cash to my children, at less than the running rate of interest, I may say, because in these days it is only right that they should have a cabin cruiser in each of their gardens or their neighbours would think their father to be an old skinflint. And only last week I gave £5 to the organ fund in this very church, and a couple of my suits to Revd. Petty. I realise there's a disparity in the sizes of us two but Revd. Petty was right, showing good Christian responsibility, in agreeing to pay the alteration costs from his stipend. None of us should look a gift horse in the mouth. This is why I resent when clients challenge the value of advice for which I have forgotten to charge a fee. What right have they to expect SOUND advice for nothing. That's what's wrong with society – it wants everything for nothing. However we only get out of life what we put into it, and I have put so much in that it would have been downright unjust had I got other than a whole lot out. Praise the Lord!

'So, dearly beloved, there you have it. The Lord giveth and the Lord taketh away. Praised be the Name of the Lord who gives bounteously to those who deserve it. And how do we deserve it? Well – that's a long story which shortage of time denies me the opportunity to expand on. However, my office is open tomorrow at nine o'clock – well, I may not be in till a little later than this for personal reasons – and it is in the silent chapel of my office room that we can talk and become aware together, pray together and find peace of mind together. All those of you with an eager heart and enquiring mind draw near thereto and we will share a real experience together.

'There is, of course, a price to pay even for spiritual fulfilment. Life is a balance sheet of debits as well as credits. This is the Lord's Will, and the Lord's Will be done. Those who would seek the Lord privately have no right to expect His blessing on the NHS, know what I mean?

'The Lord bless you and keep you and make the light of his countenance shine upon you and give you peace. Amen.'

And Duncan sat himself down grinning with self-satisfaction. Revd. Petty's head was again buried in his hands in utter terror, and he only just managed to terminate the service.

Without changing out of his fancy dress, Duncan took the long way home, along the promenade where strollers foregathered that chill November noontide. Flamboyantly swinging his crook and making the sign of the cross, he uttered a beaming 'God bless You' to each who passed him, irrespective of race, colour or seeming creed. When he got home and into polo-neck top and cord bottoms, he sat down at the dinner table and poured himself a large red wine, whilst awaiting the arrival of his soup. Raising his eyes piously to the cobwebs at the flaking cornice, he took the glass in both hands and reverentially droned 'This is the blood of Christ, who taketh away the sins of the World.'

Duncan then emptied his glass in a couple of urgent gulps, belched, and silently thanked his Maker for having inspired him, only that morning, to challenge a whole congregation with the Word of the Living God. Would that all Churches had been tuned in. Duncan waited expectantly for the phone to ring with messages of congratulation. None came. After lunch, he slept an hour or more, then, watched Jim Bowen's 'Bullseye' on television. Smashing – super!

THE FUNERAL

Shafts of sunlight peering into Duncan's Chambers between the seagull droppings on his windows sparkled on the moist stubble above his upper lip like tiny diamonds. As he breathed out, a mini-rainbow shone between his nose and where his chin, would have been if he'd got one. His glazed eyes barely focused on the scatter of waste paper with which his desk was strewn, and as he squinted his eyes across the mess, he visualised a snowscape, in which ink bottle, pens, a rubber, his specs and others became shrubs, rocks and a snow hut – and the various shadings of faded papers, files and books were no more than the light and shadow elements of the terrain over which he felt himself ski-ing à la James Bond on dangerous slopes towards the precipice which was the edge of his desk. Sensing the approaching drop, Duncan fumbled for the ripcord of the parachute which was strapped to his back, took a deep breath, and braced himself for take off.

A sharp crack like rifle fire exploded behind him – between the seat of his trousers and the plastic cover of his chair, to be exact – and Duncan cursed that second ladle of beans which had smothered his black puddings but an hour before. Pretending that he was brushing snow off his ski-pants, Duncan wafted away the stench left behind by the rifle's crack (or whatever) and then lent forward in readiness for take-off. The door opened just as he jumped off his seat, spiralling out of control behind his desk whilst shouting 'Geronimo' with a bellow that would have triggered an avalanche had the snow been real. As he gawped towards the now open door, on all fours, Virginia entered with the day's second postal delivery, enquiring if he would attend to it since both Jerry and Ray were out.

'Out, are they!' thundered Duncan, rising to his feet and scratching his bottom. 'Yes dear, leave the letters on my desk. Goodness knows when I'll get the time to look at them …'

Virginia had left before Duncan got to the 'Goodness knows' bit. She had heard it all before how that Mr Smile did all the work whilst his indolent partners swanned around.

'Bloody old fool,' Virginia whispered as she hip-swayed upstairs. Even the lowliest member of staff knew the score of which partners worked, and when, and which did not, and Duncan was left with no one to impress except himself and his suffering spouse Doreen. Mark you, Duncan must have put on a good act at home or else his wife was incredibly gullible. Mrs Smile talked non-stop and got about town to all sorts of meetings. Practically all her conversation was about her husband's overwork and poor health, and to those who were daft enough to listen, Ray and Jerry were rotters who got a good living from the efforts of their dying senior whose body and spirit were at breaking point on their account. Indeed, there were people who cut Ray and Jerry dead in the street, contemptuous of the advantage taken by them and their like of Duncan's good-natured self-sacrifice. Ray never bothered, or at least said he didn't. Jerry, however, went through phases of depression over this, during which his work tempo rose as if heightened output would smother criticism, justified or not, of his performances.

As it happens both Ray and Jerry had been out looking at different properties scheduled for adding to the firm's considerable 'Properties for Sale' column in the weekly *Bugle*, the local paper most eagerly scanned by home seekers. Each of Ray and Jerry had been successful in coaxing, the property owners to allow Messrs Chancer to handle their affairs so that, between them, prospects of a good £2,000 or more of fee income had been earned by their efforts. Both were back at their desks by 11 a.m., by which time Duncan, having been in the office only an hour since his windy breakfast, was off to the crematorium to say farewell to one of his old schoolteachers. 'Smelly' Robertson was ninety six when he was knocked off his bike by a wayward lorry, and whilst no one had a good word to say for the old bugger in his teaching days, Duncan just had to represent his class of whenever it was in honouring his highly esteemed and much loved tutor of yesteryear. Indeed, on his way to the 'Crem', Duncan's hands glowed with the pain of recalling all the beltings he had suffered at Smelly's sadistic hands, and smiled weakly as the pain subsided.

Actually, Duncan quite liked funerals and had become something of a professional mourner. He'd been known, while at the Crematorium anyway, to stay on to the next funeral if it was raining when the earlier one scaled, or if he thought the latter might offer a more sumptuous funeral tea.

Duncan almost invariably went to the funeral tea after the committal. Seldom did any of the real mourners know who he was, but five minutes into the sandwiches, Duncan had spread the word about himself, his overwork, his partners, his ill health, his earnings, his pension and investment provisions – and once everyone had shaken off the embarrassment of his company, Duncan would make a bee-line for the deceased's immediate family to smarm some valedictory praise of the deceased, then collect his coat and shamble out to his Granada, wiping from his lips with the back of his sleeve the fatty remnants of the newly partaken boiled ham sandwich, much of which was still wedged between his teeth.

To Duncan's immense pleasure, Smelly Robertson's funeral was to be a funeral lunch, and Duncan heartily accepted the Minister's invitation on behalf of the family to attend at Savaloy Hotel for refreshments and a bite to eat. At half past noon, a waiter was carrying a silver tray round the mourners laden with glasses of whisky, gin, sherry and orange juice.

'I don't usually drink during the day,' said Duncan as he lifted the fullest glass of gin on offer, 'but Mr Robertson was a very good friend to me and it would be improper to drink to his memory in anything less than 40% proof.'

The first gin was just to wet his lips. After another two which he gulped down in case the tray stopped coming, Duncan's tongue had become loosened, and his assault on the sensitivity of grieving ears went into top gear. Eventually seated, at a table for six, Duncan laid Messrs Chancer bare, unwittingly ensuring that no future clients would ever come from the ranks of those within earshot. Red wine washed down the steak pie. Red wine in carafes.

'I hate carafes,' interrupted Duncan to his table companions who were talking football. 'Never know what the damned stuff is. I'm a member of three wine clubs – mark you we don't actually drink the labels, but wine always tastes better when you've had the chance to read what's on the bottle.'

No one paid the slightest attention. Duncan began to feel a bit queasy. He had drunk too much too quickly and positively gorged himself on every morsel of the three-course lunch, plus biscuits and cheese. Half way through his Grand Marnier he felt sick and excused himself. Once out of the smoke filled restaurant of the Hotel, he felt slightly easier, but then remembered his car. He asked Reception to phone him a taxi, collected his coat, his cap and his woolly mittens and waited outside in the rain till the taxi arrived. No one bothered to follow him out to enquire for his wellbeing. In fact, there was a fair bit of 'passing by on the other side' whilst he swayed alone.

He was in bed asleep uneasily when Doreen got back from the Women's Guild at five o'clock.

In his dream Duncan was being thrashed stupid by old Smelly and thinking murderous thoughts as the fiend flailed his hands and wrists with pickled leather. Doreen's arrival at the bedside shook him from his nightmare, and he shot straight out of bed to the bathroom and discharged the contents of his funeral lunch down the loo.

When Doreen got among the members at the Indoor Bowling Club at half past six, she told how her husband was abed from a combination of nervous exhaustion and adulterated meat at the Savaloy. Expressions of sympathy were not tendered.

The morning's second mail lay unopened at the edge of Duncan's desk, whence the cleaner accidentally and unknowingly tipped it into the wastebasket before consigning the contents of the latter into a polybag for collection with the following day's refuse.

Duncan was off for two days nominally with food poisoning. The business did not suffer from his absence.

THE WEDDING

The following Thursday morning would have been the usual late mid-week anti-climax but for the fact that Duncan's daughter, Sue-Ellen, was to have her marriage solemnised two days thereafter at St. Artois Parish Church, and her not even expecting. The groom, Richard Bunting, was a high-level district athlete of greyhound dimensions. Teetotal, non-smoking, and an economist with Parliamentary ambitions. Being of the Liberal-Social Democrat persuasion, his dreams of occupying Number Ten had a hint of fantasy about them. But then Ray hadn't given up golf just because winning the 'Open' was likely to elude him.

Ray arrived at the Office at ten fifteen, looking as green as the incredible hulk – and the torn shirt added credibility to the resemblance. Miss Bottom's jeans suffered from considerable wear and tear as they stretched up and down stairs like a yo-yo ferrying black coffee conveyor-belt style.

(Electric kettles have since popped up in various parts of the office for the partners' emergency convenience though room service is still much preferred.)

Jerry had accepted an invitation to speak at Sue-Ellen's reception at the Robin Hood Hotel, and Duncan had nominated his wife Doreen to make the speech customarily delivered by the bride's father. It was the partners' hope that the business would tick over without crisis till the weekend, partly because the weather had picked up for a change, and Ray was anxious to play some forenoon golf as compensation for giving up his usual afternoon foursome on the Saturday. In fact, with the wedding ceremony set for 2 p.m. on that day, Ray would still be able to manage eighteen morning holes.

Thursday slid through without incident, but Friday was altogether a different kettle of fish. For a start, the morning mail was a mile high and contained three notable 'nasties'. Duncan's 'nasty' was not unexpected – a petition by his former client Mr Georgeson – him with the time-barred compensation claim – seeking restitution from Messrs Chancer in the sum of £12,000. Mr Georgeson, after falling out with Duncan and reporting him to the Law Society, consulted with Mr George Crudd, of the rival firm of Messrs J & G Crudd, through whose aegis this Court Summons was now served. Nothing could relieve Duncan's gloom – not even Miss Bottoms and her coffee – and he sat silently behind closed doors. Eventually, with a resigned sigh, Duncan switched on his recording machine and dictated a long incoherent letter to the Professional Indemnity Insurers, enclosing the petition, and thus abandoning the matter to their Claims' Department. He felt better with this job done, took a couple of pills, stretched his legs the length of Jerry's room. For a change, Jerry's door was shut, but this didn't muffle the sound of shouting audible to Duncan as he cocked his ear from the hallway.

Jerry's postal bombshell had had him ruminating for a good half-hour, and then he yielded to his initial impulse to get his response out of his system with a swift telephonic rejoinder. Duncan strained his ears from outside, trying to get the drift of his partner's excited expletives, but could not, of course, hear the other half of the conversation from whoever was the recipient of Jerry's vitriol. What Duncan DID hear, however, was Jerry's concluding thunder before he threw the phone back at its cradle:

'Just wait till I get my hands on that idiot Smile!'

In a single moment, Jerry leapt over his desk and yanked his door open. Duncan, who had been leaning on the door with his ear fast to the jamb, fell into the room as Jerry flew into the opening gap. Heads cracked like willow on leather, and both lawyers collapsed unconscious on to the linoleum.

Helping hands dragged the limp bodies further into Jerry's room, and laid them out on the carpet like the victims of an earthquake waiting for mass burial.

Both regained consciousness in a few minutes of ministration, feeling very sore, and drawing slowly and silently from the eternal coffee.

'What was that all about?' enquired Ray, who had now joined the small group surrounding the dazed duo.

'Your SENIOR partner, Mr Smile,' replied Jerry, 'has put us in bother to the tune of £25,000 – thanks to his bloody interference. On Tuesday afternoon, I sent out an acceptance of a £165,000 offer for Bairds'

Engineering business. And what did Mister Smile do? – He sent out an equally binding acceptance of an offer of £140,000 for the same bloody place!'

'But,' chipped in Duncan, composing himself, 'I met Fergus Baird on Monday in the off-licence, and he said he'd be happy with £140,000, and when I opened an offer for this amount on Tuesday, I decided to accept it while the going was good.'

'Fergus Baird is NOT your bloody client, Mister Smile, and when the £165,000 offer was delivered here by hand on Tuesday afternoon while YOU were sleeping off your lunch, I took the trouble to seek MY client's up-to-date instruction – and I acted in accordance with MY client's instruction. Now, I believe, both 'purchasers' want to hold us to the deal. WHY, MISTER SMILE, WHY don't you mind your own bloody business?'

Jerry's question was rhetorical, and called for no answer.

'What should we do, then?' enquired Duncan after a pause.

'What YOU should do, Mr Smile, is to have yourself declared insane – which shouldn't be difficult – but beforehand, get a letter off to our Indemnity Company and advise them that a whopping claim is in the pipeline.'

'Not another!' quivered Duncan.

'WHAT!' spat Jerry?

'Oh, never mind – just thinking aloud.' Duncan got up, rubbed his head, and announced to Mrs Mulcaster that he was going home to lie down till mid-afternoon.

Time was – 11.40 a.m.

Ray's bombshell came at twelve noon, by hand from the receptionist who had found a buff envelope lying on the floor unopened after all the morning mail had been cleared. The envelope read: 'Mrs Marjory Squeeze, c/o Messrs H.Chancer & Co.' Ray opened the envelope, ripping it to shreds in the process, and turned from green to white. At forty-eight years of age, Marjory's pregnancy test was declared positive.

Duncan came in at four o'clock, signed his mail, and left straight-way thereafter, stopping only to call through Jerry's doorway, 'See you tomorrow.'

Jerry didn't summon the courtesy of a reply, but listened as Duncan trod downstairs, heavy and alone.

Ray had left suddenly and with positively no flourish whatever the very instant he had read of Marjory's 'good news'.

He didn't come back.

Jerry left at 4.50, having explained at reception that he'd better go before anything else happened. Miss Bottoms, who had 'happened' upon the crumpled note on Ray's desk, regaled the whole office with what they referred to as 'Ray's Baby', due some eight months hence ' with a silver putter in its mouth'.

Saturday at ten to two in the afternoon saw St. Artois Parish Church with a healthy one hundred and fifty of a congregation – somewhat more than on a Sunday morning. Winter – or a hint of it – may have been just approaching, but this was the inevitable mink coat/jacket and floppy-hat affair. The heavy smell of mothballs argued with the pong of mink, unpleasant no matter how expensive. The menfolk looked as good as they could in their hired tails. Richard, the groom, and Stanley, his best man, were running-on-the-spot in front of the altar – as a concession, no doubt, to the former's fanaticism for pre-nuptial keep-fitness. Just before the bell-tower clapped 'Two', the veiled and white-clad Sue-Ellen entered from the back of the church on Duncan's arm, followed by two bridesmaids in plain but elegant lilac satin. The more stunning of the two was none other than Virginia Bottoms, a school classmate of the bride.

At ten past two, just after the 'Dearly beloved' bit, the back door swung open forcefully, its brass handle thumping the stone pillar, and in staggered Ray uttering a loud 'Sshh!' and supporting (though it should have been the other way round) Marjory's arm, guiding his beloved to a back seat with a gentleness more befitting the attention due to a lady nearer her delivery date. The top button of his shirt was undone, and his tie very squint. But his hired tails redeemed his appearance somewhat, if only from a distance. It was only when Ray pulled at his knees on sitting that Jerry, nosey enough to look round, espied Ray's red and green striped sock and spiked golf shoes, which scraped eerily on the quarry tile floor. Far from inaudibly, Ray whispered down the aisle

'Cut it a bit fine!'

As the ceremony continued, the guests tried with difficulty to ignore Ray's hiccoughs as they echoed from the arched roof.

There's one thing that hardened drinkers, social drinkers and non-drinkers all agree upon, and that is that free champagne at a wedding is most acceptable. And, about three glasses ahead at the Robin Hood Hotel, everyone – even the crabbit ones – were in fairly high spirits. The cake cut, eaten, and praised with the customary hypocrisy, the gathering set about the usual indifferent meal and some quite appalling wines of both white and red varieties – just the right kind to serve after the palates have already been dulled – if not actually destroyed – by the champagne and whatever else has been dispensed over the bar. The Quids and Squeezes were at the same table, and Ray's attentiveness towards his wife was something to be seen – partly on account of her condition, but mostly as grovelling compensation for the state in which he had got home from the morning's golf. A few drinks on, and before the speeches commenced, Ray stood up and called for silence.

'I'm going to have a baby!' he announced, then fell back on his chair with a huge grin. Before Marjory had a chance to tell him to shut up, the local G.P. got to his feet offering his services, and also those of the midwife, co-incidentally in attendance at the next table in her capacity as aunt of the bride. The wedding guests found the incident mildly amusing, and were grateful for some light relief, noting from the Toast List that the formal speeches promised precious little in the way of entertainment.

Reverend Petty got to his feet, and, with a brevity which so often eludes those called to the 'cloth', welcomed the assembled company, offered on behalf of everyone heartiest congratulations and good wishes to the new Mr and Mrs Bunting, and invited that we should all rise and drink the health of the happy couple. Calls of 'Good Health', 'Cheers', and 'God Bless' filled that part of the air not choked out with smoke. The Revd. sat down, and Richard got up.

'On behalf of my wife and myself ...(applause)...I thank you all for your attendance, and for your gifts, and for your kind thoughts; I thank my parents for all their care during my single state, and Sue-Ellen's parents for their gift of my lovely wife. You are all welcome to our new home at 18 Veronica Gardens – but not all at the one time please … (applause) … I can't tell you where we are going on our honeymoon, because my in-laws would probably arrive there ahead of us! But I'll give you a clue to the kind of holiday – we're changing into track-suits before we leave here….'

'I hope you're joking, dearest,' interrupted Sue-Ellen, laying down her whisky-glass and drawing on a long cigar.

'Oh course I'm joking, my love,' the groom continued, 'but we're going to a non-licensed Hotel, and you are taking no smokes with you!'

Cries of 'Shame' leapt from all tables.

'I think that's all I have to say. Thanks again!' Richard concluded.

'I think he's said too ruddy much, if you ask me,' said Jerry to Ray. 'I don't think it's a good idea to criticise the bride this early in the marriage, especially in front of an audience.'

There were uneasy murmurings at the top table, as Sue-Ellen jumped up with her eyes aflame and slapped her new husband resoundingly across the face.

'Quite right, dearie,' shouted Mrs Gow, one of Ray's most aggravating clients, a guest of the bride. 'Sort the bugger out from the start, that's the way.'

Revd. Petty stood up and asked for calm. When all was silent, Mr Petty raised his eyes, closed them theatrically, bowed his head, and, with proper ecclesiastical voice, boomed out –

'Our Father in Heaven, grant that Thy blessing and loving Spirit shall enter into all our hearts; heal the wounds open by unkind words and deeds. Teach us tolerance and understanding, and especially guard Richard and Sue-Ellen from anything which might spoil, even a little, the new lives to be shared, each with the other. For Thy Name's sake we ask these things. Amen.'

Richard and Sue-Ellen had joined hands under the table, and smiled lovingly at each other as Reverend Petty re-took his seat.

'Damned effective prayer, that,' said Ray on seeing such patent evidence of the young couple's reconciliation.

Doreen was next on her feet, and, to save the reader's boredom, let it be said that she read from notes prepared by Duncan in what must have been one of his blackest bouts of manic depression. It was all about the loss of a daughter, the split – nae, the destruction – of the Smile family. The poor woman even read the concluding four words of her husband's notes,

'Yours faithfully, Duncan Smile.'

A shuffle of unease disturbed the silence as Jerry rose to speak, specially among those who didn't have Jerry marked down as too diplomatic.

'Reverend Petty, Richard and Sue-Ellen, Duncan and Doreen, and fellow Guests – I couldn't get tickets for the Heavyweight Boxing Match, but this has been just as good!'

During the momentary embarrassed silence which followed Jerry's opening salvo, Duncan's right hand stretched out under the top table for something to hold on to and the only object to hand was the knee of the bridesmaid at his side, Miss Bottoms. The silence enabled her 'Not now, Mr Smile' to reach all corners of the dining room, so, as Jerry went on, the atmosphere, even without the smoke, was very cuttable.

'But seriously, folks,' trying to redeem the situation, 'What a happy occasion, and how lucky we all are to share in the launching of a new family. And isn't it so refreshingly honest that we can all act naturally on such a day as this. So often, wedding receptions are so formal, so polite, so stuffy – and so DULL! People feel obliged to say the 'right' things, and to behave with such uncharacteristic propriety that the whole affair looks like a bad amateur play, so strained and artificial are all the actors in their over-rehearsed efforts to impress their relations in the audience. Not so with us, friends – isn't it delightful to see newlyweds *so* much in love that they can even afford to share their first tantrum – out in the open, among friends …'

Relieved smiles were risked here and there.

'… And even Duncan can light-heartedly fumble Miss Bottoms the bridesmaid. What does that say about Duncan and Doreen? It says that they are so loving and devoted to each other, so wholly trusting and in tune together – and with us, their affectionate friends – that Duncan can indulge in a little humorous side-show without losing an ounce of the regard in which he is held by us all. For they, truly, are jolly good fellows ...'

And the guests drowned out anything that was left with an off-key rendering of the well-known song, sung in relaxed sincerity, and followed by a thundering vote of thanks.

Reverend Petty called an interval, and the party split into the customary two files, one for the toilets and the other for the Cocktail Lounge. Marjory pulled Ray to one side before they separated to the former and the latter respectively, and warned, 'We have a solid and loving marriage, Ray, but that doesn't mean you can grope the bridesmaid, got it?'

'No, love of my life,' Ray slurred. 'It might spoil my putting!'

Marjory's warning was not too inappropriate. About forty husbands had drawn their wives to one side and told them how much in love they were with their very own spouses – then spent the rest of the evening hovering around the bridesmaids, and the other young things who arrived later on for the dancing. Glasses of brandy and Babycham were thrust into any young female hand. The wives were less fortunate.

The Reverend, who had been on orange juice throughout the formalities, yielded to 'hospitality' during the two-hour dance, and was last seen in the kitchen conducting a seeming 'marriage' of two waiters, neither of whom had bothered to shave for the event.

Richard and Sue-Ellen left on a tandem at 9 p.m. in a flood of confetti and tears.

At midnight, Duncan and Doreen held each other close, surrounded by the Auld Lang Syners. The Hotel at last empty, the two newly married waiters came into the Function Suite to survey the mass of bottles, glasses, plates, cups, ashtrays and debris.

'Oh, it's our first night, Stewart – let's leave the washing up till the morning, and go to bed.'

'Good idea, Lewis,' replied the 'bride'.

And they headed for the stairs, killing the lights on the way.

APRÈS-NUPTIALS – THE MONDAY FOLLOWING

There's a snag about most days.

As Ray says – 'I hate Fridays – next thing you know it's Monday!'

Of course, it's true. If you haven't done it, or whatever, on a Friday night, you wake up the next day and there's only Sunday separating you from bleedin' Monday. All very depressing.

But, in a way, Messrs Smile, Quid and Squeeze (if not those who work for them) quite look forward to Monday. Especially Jerome Lenza Quid as he climbs the antiseptic atmosphere of the stone and tiled staircase at 8.45 a.m., bundle of unopened mail underarm, and still having smoked none. Door open and lights on. Coat off, gas fire on. Eighty-odd assorted envelopes on a clear counter. Toledo steel opener in right hand and first fag of the day in the other. A hefty load of mysteries ready for slashing into the reality of a new week. No one is due in the office for at least ten minutes. Taken with the excitement of it all, Jerry dashes to the loo for a violent crap and wash-up. Must be comfy for the occasion or the thrill of expectancy would be spoiled. Just as players filing out on to the Wembley turf for a Cup Final daren't have to rush back to the bog, so Jerry must have everything just right for the big opening.

Just as Abraham raised the knife prepared to sacrifice Isaac, so Jerry – eventually, all things just right – raises his Toledo, and cuts through a buff coloured envelope, and reads …

'Dear Sirs,

We are delighted to invite you to an exhibition of electronic data-processors at the County Hotel on …'

'Piss off!' mutters Jerry, slinging the missive into the bucket.

The next envelope in foolscap has a nice 'feel' to it, and the letter is headed 'International Building Contractors' and reads –

'We have acquired four hundred acres of prestigious land near to your township (Plan attached) with Planning Permission in detail for the erection of three thousand detached dwellinghouse units of executive category and choice of forty individual designs. Our policy is to employ local lawyers to act for us in the promotion and sale of such. Might you be interested in acting as our agents in this development …?'

'Too bloody right we would!' shouted Jerry as Zoë passed the counter on entering.

Another uncharacteristic week had dawned.

OFFICE REFURBISHMENT

Old Henry Chancer himself, who died in 1975, was a tall gaunt figure with a squarish bald head flanked by bushy white curls overhanging pointed ears and the collar of his Tootal shirt. A grey Groucho Marx moustache and horn-rimmed glasses comprised his facial adornment, along with the thin lips of a man not prone to excessive generosity. Probably because of his broad shoulders, height and fat free bone structure, his suits always looked a couple of sizes too large for him. And the brown brogues with which his feet were invariably clad looked like a pair from a bout of bulk buying (for economy, of course) in the mid-thirties.

Henry's off-duty obsession was horse-racing, and not as a rider either – as a voyeur and a backer. And the proximity of one of the country's front-line racecourses was a real delight to old Henry, a long-time member there to whom privileges of parking and 'executive' facilities applied and were wholesomely used. It might have been difficult to coax a penny out of Henry's purse at the office, but at the racecourse he had a justifiable reputation as one of the most generous gentlemen on God's earth. His financial faith in the unlikeliest of nags was boundless, as also his willingness to pick up the tab for the liquid après-post, win or lose.

In Henry's day, the walls of the office waiting room were broken by several prints of misshapen horses, such as painted by Alfred Munnings, in his ill-conceived attempt to portray racehorses at the gallop. The day after Henry's funeral, his family had spent an hour with Duncan ostensibly to discuss the winding up of the deceased lawyer's estate, then physically removed the Munnings' prints from the waiting room on their way out. They also took old Henry's will with them so as to instruct other lawyers to do the business, all to the astonishment of Duncan's partners. Duncan dribbled some story about 'conflict of interest, you know – wouldn't have been right for us to be involved …'

'Utter crap, you fool,' Ray pounced. 'These Johnnies who wind up the old bastard's estate will want access to all our bloody facts and figures.

Not that they'll need them, of course – just to satisfy their friggin curiosity.'

In truth, Duncan had made no such conflict of interest suggestion to the Chancer family members. Rather, Duncan had gabbed about how lucky the Chancers would be to get anything out of a business to which the deceased had contributed so little. Not unnaturally the Chancers took offence and told Duncan a few home truths of their own, and the meeting had collapsed in mutual contempt and the flood of Mrs Chancer's tears. Hence their removal of the prints and the removal of their business and the end of thirty years of connection with the very firm that old Henry had started with nothing but hope.

Now, there is really no point in making mention of this episode so late in our narrative, except to explain that, four years on, there are still fade marks on the waiting room walls to vouch where the prints once hung. Such has been the fastidiousness of old Henry's successors. Mark you, only yesterday Jerry suggested that the waiting room area, perhaps even among others, could do with a freshen up.

'Waste of time and money,' replied Ray. 'The clients will just rub their greasy coats on the fresh distemper and make it look even worse.'

'Distemper!!' astonished Jerry. 'Where have you been all these years? No one uses distemper any more.'

'I do – I found a bag in the washhouse last weekend and have just re-done the lounge at home,' boasted Ray.

Jerry grimaced and dared not say anything more on the topic, but still thought how positively spendthrift had been old Henry when compared to Mr Squeeze. Closing his door on re-entering his own room, Jerry lit a cigarette and wondered when, or even whether, it would ever be possible to drag his partnership into the twentieth century – or even the nineteenth century. There's no way in which to get three people thinking in unison. God knows about these big city partnerships with a score or more involved. Clearly, they must delegate different jobs to different partners – maybe a 'fabric partner' could blitz the office without consulting any of the partners except the one called 'budget?

As for Chancers, and despairing of uncoerced agreement, Jerry fell back on a 'memo' to the others. But what about appropriate wording?

How to appeal to Duncan? How to appeal to Ray? After half filling the waste bucket with discarded ideas, the memo for issue read as follows:-

MEMO FOR PARTNERS

As is clear to our Staff and our clients, if not yet to ourselves, our premises, furnishings, fittings and decoration are getting tired after some thirty years of neglect. On the basis that (from past experience) a general refurbishment programme now will relieve us of capital expenditure for the *next* thirty years, it is proposed:-

(a) To redecorate one room at a time starting at the attic and ending at the front door.
(b) To re-carpet the office in the same sequence.
(c) To refurnish the partners' rooms.
(d) To renew all partners' cars.
(e) To award partners an extra two weeks annual holiday.
(f) To award each partner an immediate £1000 in cash as a tax-free allowance to cover business entertaining.
(g) To meet as partners after working hours once per month to discuss business matters and to ensure that agreed refurbishment continues apace to its satisfactory conclusion.
Signed J.L.Q.

Jerry passed his memo to each of his partners who responded with commendable haste, indicating approval of items (d) (e) and (f) only, the others being deleted in thick black marker pens.

Jerry frowned sourly. Partnership, he mused, is like democracy. It doesn't work, though it's probably better than whatever is its alternative. Well, maybe…

As it happens, a measure of refurbishment was forced on the partners as the result of a visit by two gentlemen only a week later.

THE ENVIRONMENTAL MEN

Subsequent to the passing of the Offices Shops and Railway Premises Act, law offices, among others, have come under the scrutiny of the authorities. It is easy to imagine how law offices have offered some raw meat to the Inspectors, more so than, for example, Insurance Companies, who, like Building Societies, Banks and Estate Agents – or some of them – either have the money to up-date their premises or else respond to the need to present a modern commercially efficient looking front to attract business. Lawyers, at this stage in our narrative, barred from advertising their wares, have tended to rely on expertise and repute – or native cunning – for their commercial end product. Their premises, frequently in unprepossessing tenements (though this is, at long last, undergoing change) have not been the subject of over much notice by officialdom, or by anyone else. After all, they have never been known as beauty spots, and the public in general has been loath to enter their portals for fear of being rendered with an extortionate bill. So, not infrequently, Law Offices *are* the cream, brown and black dustheaps as depicted in faded Victorian drawings and sepia etchings.

Messrs Chancers' offices might not have been quite in the relegation zone of the solicitors' league table, but neither were they challenging for promotion to a higher order of things. It took the arrival, unannounced, one morning, of Mr Gongby and Mr Tombworth to awaken the partners' dull senses to the following list of noted demerits:-

ENTRANCE HALL

(a) Linoleum worn through showing gaps in floorboards, hazardous, particularly for ladies in high heels.
(b) Electric light switches and plugs loose and dangerous and coupled with half-inch dust clinging to walls constitutes fire hazard.
(c) Cracked and sellotaped glass in Reception Area, dangerous and needing renewal; nails sticking out of counter at public side thereof.
(d) No ventilation, and 60 watt bulb inadequate to light two thousand cubic feet.

(e) Ceiling badly cracked and in seemingly dangerous condition.
(f) No smoke doors, no fire extinguisher, no thermometer and no First Aid Kit.

So, before actually getting to any part of the office proper, the report was shaping up poorly, and the remainder of the office was scheduled to fare even worse. What was said about the toilets, washing and recreation facilities would have filled a chapter each.

Mr Tombworth did the talking, and Mr Gongby carried the clipboard and a great sheaf of paper as if in the expectancy that a great sheaf would be necessary. Both were dressed like 1920s men from the Pru', and neither seemed capable of smiling. It was lunchtime before they reached Duncan's room, by which time Duncan was at home savouring the bouquet of the Chianti with which he planned to wash down a plate of beans on toast.

Tombworth and Gongby stopped in their unemotional tracks as they entered the chamber, which bore the senior partner's name. Tin deed boxes, bundles of property deeds, files, books and general litter took up about half of the floor space, and the furnishings much that was left. Gongby's clipboard began to twitch with anticipation.

'Right, Gongby, get noting,' said his superior.

'I. Ancient gas heating appliance; ill fitting windows sealed with sellotape, incapable of being opened; each undesirable, and together a positive danger.
II. Frayed electric light cord strung to one side to allow light (grossly inadequate) at desk.
III. Worn carpet at door and round desk toward window, with loose cords bound to induce tripping.
IV. So dark, light meter registers nothing.
V. No ventilation; oppressive smell of gas, body odour and anal wind.
VI. Traces of dampness on all walls.
VII. Positively insanitary.
VIII. Notify re-inspection fourteen days hence to see marked improvement or recommend steps toward closure.'

'Is that all, sir?' enquired Gongby.

'I wouldn't be certain of that,' replied Tombworth. 'There's so little of this damned place not covered with junk.'

Tombworth slipped the toe of his worn and out-dated winkle-picker under a bundle of title deeds and flicked them up in the air. The perished rubber band with which they were held together snapped in the process and about twenty deeds fell to rest at random over an area of three square yards of unfilled – and probably unread and unanswered – letters.

'Shall I pick these up, sir?' trembled Gongby.

'Will you hell!' shot Tombworth. 'Serve the bugger right if it takes him a year to sort them out. Let's get out of here before I throw up!'

And the two gents left without any more flourish than that with which they had arrived.

Responding to the recorded delivery 'get sorted out or else' letter, which arrived after only forty-eight hours of waiting, tradesfolk took residence for a couple or more weeks, and Messrs Chancers' league rating improved a few notches within the month. They didn't bother redecorating, however, the reason being advanced that old was dignified whereas new was flash.

Of course, the partial tidying-up process meant that none of the partners could find anything without a prolonged search. So, at a cost of some £5,000, Messrs Smile, Quid and Squeeze spent the most part of yet another month looking for this and that which, hitherto, had been readily to hand from one or another heap of dollops in their respective domains.

As blood pressures rise, and tempers snap, does the self-employed professional taxpayer raise his bloodshot eyes to Heaven and thank God for the intervention of His Almighty Civil Servants who so enrich his lot?

Ray was the one with the succinct, if not wholly diplomatic, summary:-

'Bet the bastards are paid a bloody fortune of public money in order to do bugger-all else than snarl up anything that looks like private enterprise. And, with their cost-of-living indexed bloody pensions in sight after they have bankrupted folk like us, no wonder the swine are on the waiting-lists of every up-market Golf Club in the friggin' country!'

The changing face of Britain. Where are, indeed, the remaining bastions of exclusivity – where 'decent' people can hide away from those whom 'progress' hath elevated?

SIGNS OF SUMMER – THE GOLF OUTING

The routine ceremony of opening the morning mail came to an abrupt and smiling halt. Jerry discarded the torn envelope and held up a stencilled letter – but not the usual waste-bucket circular. Something special. A fresh fag lit, Jerry read excitedly:-

Faculty of Solicitors
ANNUAL GOLF OUTING
To
WESTERN GOLF COURSE
Wednesday 18th June at 08.30 a.m.

Please indicate whether to attend for:
Morning Coffee……………………

Morning Singles
Sheriff Shoelace Cup………………
Lunch – 1.20 p.m.…………………

Afternoon foursomes
2.30 onwards………………………
Evening Meal – 7.30………………
Prizegiving – 8.30…………………

Carriages – Midnight.

'That's next Wednesday,' whistled Jerry softly, rushing through the rest of the letters, then slumping into his desk chair and swinging his feet on to the desk in a single, well-practised movement. The rest of the mail lay unattended as Jerry read the circular another half-dozen times, on each occasion conjuring up a new joyous shot to flagstick after flagstick on his way to a record score. Asked to indicate which parts of the outing he was to attend, Jerry answered in the affirmative, from Morning Coffee to Carriages.

FRIDAY THE THIRTEENTH

Ray clocked in at 9.22 a.m. and threw his plastic anorak into a corner. He looked in a foul mood. The yolk of a soft boiled egg – or, a fair bit of it – had hardened into his tie and left lapel, and his hair spoke of a wet and windy trip across the car park, or gross neglect, or both. He grabbed at his phone and yelled at Mrs Mulcaster that he wanted no interruptions.

Unaware of Ray's ill humour, Jerry picked up the Golf Invitation and sailed breezily into Ray's Office.

'What the hell do YOU want?' snapped Ray without looking up from his desk.

Somewhat taken aback, Jerry had, however, seen this kind of mood before. Wrongly, he chose to defuse the situation with a light response –

'Who's a right jolly boy this morning, then?'

'Piss off, Mister Quid!' blasted Ray, pointing a shaky finger towards his door. Jerry accepted the invitation to leave, and left.

'Nice one, Raymond,' whispered Jerry to himself as he returned chastened to his room, closed his door and worked solidly till noon.

Miss Bottoms obviously thought Jerry's shut door meant that he was to be left undisturbed, so he missed his morning tea, and the customary two coffees with which this was usually washed down. Taking his dictated tapes and correspondence upstairs to the typists' grotto, he met on the landing Duncan coming into work sharp at 12.05 p.m.

'Friday the bloody thirteenth,' thundered Duncan. 'Just been at the doctor's – been told to take things a shade easier.'

'That will test your ingenuity, mate!' shot Jerry as he rounded the stair.

'Damned impertinence,' muttered Duncan, as he slammed his office door behind him. Puzzled by an odd smell after a few minutes in the confines of his room, Duncan paced around, sniffing here and there. The mystery solved itself when the astute lawyer saw the healthy fresh stains on his carpet, and then examined the insteps of his size tens.

'Bloody dog dirt – no wonder Law Offices are called Chambers!'

Duncan looked at the handkerchief he had removed to cover his nose, saw that it was already filthy, and started to rub the marks off, or into, the carpet.

Ray burst in, his face white and lips drawn.

'I'm going home, Duncan. My stomach's in a hell of a mess.'

That was all that Ray had come to announce, but, confused by Duncan's antics on the floor, he took a step into the room. He just saw Duncan's handkerchief when his nostrils caught the familiar scent. This, coupled with his own queasiness, induced an automatic response, and that much of Ray's breakfast which was not clinging to his clothes exploded on to Duncan's desk

To describe the scene as confused would be on the euphemistic side, and when Mrs Mulcaster phoned through to tell him that the Reverend Petty was in for his appointment, Duncan steadied himself, and announced –

'Tell the Reverend gentleman to bugger off!'

With seeming total composure, Duncan replaced the telephone receiver gently, pausing only momentarily to remove a blob of something from the mouthpiece. Turning to Ray, whose ashen jowls were set into a faint smile, Duncan mused –

'I've heard you say you're sick of this place, but THIS is ridiculous!'

Miss Bottoms was sent out for air freshener, tissues and cologne, and by one o'clock, something akin to normality had been restored. Ray was feeling the better of his gastric gut-out and much better still after a couple of very large gin and tonics at the club. Indeed, his first visit on his return to the office was to Jerry's room, wearing a broad grin, to enquire –

'Now then, old boy – I think you wanted to see me about something. Now, you know me – always ready to listen to a chum!'

Duncan spent a very argumentative lunch with his wife Doreen, who was blamed for the dog dirt, the consequences thereof, and for the loss of Revd. Petty as a client.

Not that Mrs Mulcaster would allow the last of these to happen. She had told the clergyman that Mr Smile had taken ill suddenly, and the three persons in the waiting room with him had sat with heads bowed whilst the Reverend broke into an extempore prayer, calling on Almighty God 'to grant Thy servant, Mr Smile, a speedy and full recovery to health so that the good Lawyer can continue steadfastly to uphold that which is good and true, to the advancement of Thy Kingdom on Earth – for Thy Name's sake we ask these things, AMEN.'

MONDAY THE SIXTEENTH

Ray spent most of his weekend at the Golf Club. No one at the office believed his blethers about the Lawyers' Golf Outing being a bore. Ray was as keen as mustard to get his name engraved on the Shoelace Cup for the fourth time. Jerry had managed this feat twice – twice more than Duncan – but Ray had graciously put Jerry's successes down to an inflated handicap, a poor turnout of competitors, and Ray's absence on holiday on both occasions.

When Miss Bottoms had departed Ray's room at 1030 a.m., leaving behind two steaming coffees, a trace of seductive scent, and two racing heartbeats, Jerry remarked-

'I gather you've been putting in a heap of practice over the weekend. Fancy yourself to win on Wednesday?'

'Might not go this year,' he lied in response. 'I enjoy my golf, and I can play when I want and pick my company. It's no pleasure for me to waste a day playing with a bunch of hackers – specially that jumped-up lot of youngsters who fancy themselves God's gift to the profession.'

'Be fair, Ray – none of us endeared ourselves that much to our seniors when WE were young – yet they played with US. Can't have been much fun for them whilst WE bragged ourselves out of popularity. Some of the young ones are quite pleasant, and they can only get nicer as they get older. And, in any event, we'll get a good 'bevvy' at lunchtime, which should make them ALL nice chaps by the afternoon!'

The strain vanished from Ray's face at the mention of refreshment, then tightened again.

'We'll need a damned good refreshment at lunchtime if we're to get through the kind of afternoon I had last year. Remember I got stuck with two of J & G Crudd's lot AND that old cheat Logan. Four hours wading through whins, scouring the beach and the railway-line looking for the kind of balls a dog had chewed. I was that ruddy knackered when I got back to mid-fairway each time for my own shot – small wonder I didn't win!'

'Come on, Ray – you weren't on the fairway ALL the time. The only time I saw you play, you shanked so badly I thought you had hit the ball on your backswing!'

'Now, I've told you before – a shank is only a whisker off being a perfect shot – though I have to admit that's not much of a consolation at the time.'

The phone rang its shrill intrusion into this heavy business.

'Mrs Gow on the phone, Mr Squeeze,' sniggered the telephonist.

'Tell her I died last night,' drawled Ray.

When Ray got home that evening, his hallway was adorned with the most beautiful spray of gladioli, to which a card was attached 'WITH DEEPEST SYMPATHY'.

'When's the funeral, darling?' beamed his wife.

'Shut up!' snapped Ray.

BAD DREAMS – STILL THE SIXTEENTH

Let it be understood that as with all general practitioners, Law Firms take all kinds of business. Solicitors, as individuals, have their weak as well as their strong subjects. But they don't turn down, for example, a maritime dispute, just because they haven't a clue where to start. Lawyers have to give the impression that they understand the problem, and then buy the time (with the client's money) within which to swat up on the subject. When the client doesn't give the necessary time, the lawyer has to call up his latent thespian talents, and give a performance equal to the occasion. This isn't really dishonest – any more than we'd think a medical practitioner dishonest to treat as best he can an ailment which he can't positively identify. In any event, a good lawyer doesn't allow himself to be boxed into a corner. If a problem is unduly complex, or beyond the lawyer's scope, he's perfectly entitled to refuse a hasty or ill-considered opinion. He tells the client, if need be, that the client will just HAVE to be patient if he wants his business the subject of proper consideration.

It was behind such a smokescreen that Ray always hid if approached on any topic likely to land up in court. Ray's idea of a nightmare (aside from shanking at the eighteenth in the last round of the 'Open') was to be left on his own in court with a client's whole destiny in his sweat-soaked palm.

Whether it was ruminating over his 'funeral' or some other morbidity, or the after-effects of four slices of toasted cheese, washed down by three pints of 'heavy', Ray's sleep seem destined to be a disturbed one. The dream started off cheerily enough. The local banker had consulted with him about a rape case. The good banker was alleged to have raped his own mother-in-law. The banker, one Hedley Coote, out on bail, was due for trial in a month's time. 'Phew,' thought Ray, 'A month is years away – plenty of time to get a good defence Counsel.' But dreams do not pay much attention to time, and, in a twinkling, Ray found himself in the most austere stone-pillared courtroom with an arched and beamed ceiling, stained glass windows and a dank, musty dampness about the wooden benches and flagstones, and walls dripping with condensation. On an elevated dais sat the judge, grey-wigged, with red gowns edged with ermine. The Judge's face was lined and ugly with a no-mercy look, and the jury, in rows at the side, were all fancily attired, some with grotesque faces and rouged cheeks looking, to all intents and purposes like guests at the Mad Hatter's Tea Party. The foreman, who had a horse's head and glasses, kept winking at Ray, which had the lawyer thinking that at least one of the jury was benignly disposed toward him.

Hedley was in the dock – an oaken construction with iron spikes rising some two feet from the box and then curling in menacingly about the banker's temples. In the witness-box, the victim of the alleged rape, Mrs Coote's mother, hampered with overweight, podgy-faced, and by no means a characteristic candidate for male interest, was being questioned by the prosecutor, a tall beanpole of a man, draped in black from head to toe to match his hair, his eyes and his moustache.

'And the accused,' he concluded, 'took you by force in the conservatory and left you half-naked in the dahlias?'

'Yes, Your Majesty,' replied the lady. 'It was awful...quite awful – ask my daughter, she knows what it's like. He's got a breath like he's been eating dogdirt!'

The prosecutor sat down, and the lady was about to leave the witness-box when called back by the judge.

'Just a minute, perhaps the defence lawyer will wish to ask you a few questions – Mr Squeeze?'

Ray felt rivulets of water run down his clammy back, and beads of perspiration filtered through his brows and smarted his eyes. His legs trembled violently as he invited them to take his weight. He looked for inspiration to the cobwebbed ceiling, glanced at the jury – now barely visible, having taken on the form of grinning pygmies – then at the judge, who hadn't changed. After fumbling through his sodden and indecipherable notes, Ray rubbed, and then raised, his bloodshot eyes to the witness-box, and found himself transfixed in the gaze of Mrs Gow, whose surplus flesh cascaded over a greyish corselet. The stare of the lady was defiant and nasty, and Ray's mind was a turmoil of whirling ideas, none of which could reach his lips.

'Get on with it, Mr Squeeze!' thundered the Judge, donning a black cap.

'What was it you said happened, madam?' stuttered the lawyer.

'You done me for ten bloody pounds for these flowers, you bastard!' spat Mrs Gow.

'What has that got to do with Hedley Coote?' enquired Ray.

'That's damn-all to do with you, Squeeze, but if you MUST know, I borrowed the ten nicker from the swine's bank.'

'Was it at that time that Mr Coote interfered with you?'

'Interfered my arse, Squeeze, – I wouldn't let that bloody creep near me!'

Ray smiled, and turned towards the judge, and asked for acquittal. God, the Judge was now his wife Marjory.

'YOU,' snarled Marjory, 'If it wasn't Coote, it must have been YOU who raped the banker's mother-in-law then. You will go to prison for ten years!'

'Can I go to a prison near a golf course, Your Ladyship?' enquired Ray.

Marjory's answer was a sharp elbow jabbed directly into his left eye-socket, and Ray woke and shot upright in the one instant yelling in pain and covering the left of his face with both hands. Marjory was in the middle of apologising to her agonised husband when the bedside phone rang. She took the call. Ray's wife replaced the receiver a few moments later.

'That was the police, Ray. Apparently someone's been taken into custody for raping Coote the banker's mother-in-law, and wants you to take the case.'

'Not again!' mumbled Ray as he wandered through to the lounge cabinet for some nerve tonic, and from there to the bathroom to shower away the courtroom smells.

Duncan's customary dream saw him in London's Dorchester attending as a Guest of Honour at a Film Industry Champagne Reception. Showbusiness luminaries, living and dead, each a household name, jostled without any finesse whatever just to be close to Sir Duncan Smile CBE. Duncan sipped his champagne as to the manner born, chatting with equal facility and devastating wit to superstars, deposed monarchs, cabinet ministers, fieldmarshalls and archbishops – and starlets who got within earshot giggled out of their cleavage at positively anything which Duncan uttered. In fact, Duncan eventually yielded to the clamour, and stood on a gold lamé couch so that he could be seen by more of the eager throng. To do so, he had to wave away disdainfully an excited Burt Reynolds, who sought explanation of Duncan's secret skill with women.

'Your Majesties, My Lords, Ladies and Gentlemen,' he beamed, 'how delighted I am to afford you all this opportunity of meeting me. You have to thank Sidney Greenstreet and Douglas Fairbanks – Senior, of course – for getting me here. I met Mary Pickford in Paris last night, and she reminded me that I owed Douglas a favour dating back to our boyhood when he saved me from a killer shark off Madagascar when I took cramp whilst swimming eight miles off-shore. Sidney, of course, is an old friend whom I promised to look up when next in the city.'

Carol Lombard and Veronica Lake started to fight right in front of Duncan, but did not even slightly disturb his eloquent flow.

'Now then, girls, take it easy – I'll give you a memento shortly. Perhaps something from my monogrammed underwear collection ...'

The ladies stopped fighting, as if pacified, but each held on to one of Duncan's thighs just to make sure he didn't get away.

A sudden crash at the far end of the suite had everyone turning round to behold King Kong walking through the wall – bricks cascading everywhere – cradling Fay Wray in his arms, and announcing –

'Sir Duncan's breakfast!'

Kong beat an unhurried path through the panic-stricken crowd, and stopped in front of Duncan, now in spotlit isolation on the couch.

'Your breakfast, Sir Duncan,' repeated Kong, and laid Fay gently on the carpet at his feet. Fay got up, tried to smooth down her frayed and torn dress and replace her exposed bosom, and pleaded –

'Don't eat me yet, please, Sir Duncan. Couldn't we maybe go up to my suite and discuss – er – the situation?'

'Capital!' exclaimed Duncan enthusiastically – blowing a kiss to Rita Hayworth, and placing an arm round Fay's fragile shoulder.

Once in Fay's room – a sumptuous apartment in true Hollywood tradition – four-poster, silk drapes, tinted mirrors, cascades of fresh flowers, Chinese vases and carpets, marble floors and pillars – the whole shebang – cut-crystal cocktail cabinet, roaring log fire in heavy antique surround, gold cornicing – the LOT! – the actress slipped off her dress and glided naked with sensuous grace towards the adjoining bathroom, waving a slim white arm as she smiled Duncan into total assurance of her imminent return. Duncan hurriedly undressed as he listened to the shower cascading off Fay's tingling body, poured and sank an immense brandy from the cabinet, cast an admiring glance at himself in a gilt-framed full-length mirror, and contemplated his forthcoming physical destruction with un-inhibited satisfaction.

'Who's a pretty boy, then?' he whistled, as the bathroom door opened slowly. Duncan closed his eyes as if in fervent prayer, and when he opened them again, in a frenzy of anticipation, there stood Doreen in anorak and ill-fitting simulated leopard-skin stretch trousers, taking in Duncan's nakedness with undisguised shock.

'Good God, woman, what the hell are YOU doing here?' shouted Duncan.

'I live here dear – I'm your wife, remember?'

Duncan snapped on the light and looked round the familiar shabbiness of his bedroom.

'Last time I eat that bloody toasted cheese of yours for supper, Doreen,' said the lawyer uneasily, and fell asleep clutching at his indigestion.

Jerry tried not to dream any night, in case it was the familiar one about the police officer asking him to blow in the bag.

TUESDAY THE SEVENTEENTH

'Marjory!' shouted Ray as he shambled out of bed at 8.45 a.m. 'Where's my yellow socks?'

Marjory Squeeze left her third batch of pancakes on the griddle and answered her husband's summons to the bedroom.

'You're wearing them, you idiot – I'm not surprised you forgot to take them off last night, the state you were in. How on earth did you get home?'

'Home from where?'

'Good God, man, you were golfing for a change last night – don't you remember? It was a diesel engine that stopped outside just before you fell in the front door …'

'Oh, a taxi, yes, that's right. I remember now, I was invited to someone's house late on for snooker, and couldn't say no, or leave early. It wouldn't have been polite.'

'Always the gentleman, my Raymond – wouldn't dream of being impolite to the boys,' she snarled. 'Go and have a shower and then let's see who we can send out to work this morning!'

Ray obeyed, and Marjory returned to her now smoke-filled kitchen to repair the damage to her charred griddle.

At quarter to ten, in his best suit, Ray entered the office like the proverbial new pin, feeling a lot better than he deserved, phoned Miss Bottoms for a coffee, called Jerry in for a blether, and spilled the contents of a full ink bottle over the will which lay on his blotter. The will had a note attached, which read –

'Miss Bowyer died this morning – her executor Commander Bowyer will be in to see you about the attached will at 10.30'

All of a sudden Ray felt ill again.

'What the hell do I do about *this*?' Ray asked in despair, pointing at the mess.

'Send it to the laundry, mate!' quipped Jerry.

'Be serious, man – what do *we* DO about this?'

'The clever girl who got the will from the safe photocopied it, see?' smiled Jerry, prodding beneath the soiled document towards its pristine facsimile.

'Thank God!' said Ray earnestly. 'I'll give the old boy a copy and tell him the original is in confidential keeping, or some crap like that.'

'Fair enough,' replied Jerry. 'And that will give us some time to work out the next move.'

'Super!' Ray cheered, raised his coffee cup in salute, cast a glance toward the window and saw the sun was shining. 'Might manage a few holes this afternoon!'

Jerry winced and left. Commander Bowyer was in the waiting room, red-cheeked, belligerent, plus-foured and be-monocled.

'Hello, Quid!' bellowed the Commander. 'A word in your ear before I see Squeeze. That will he's got – it's not the last one, y'know – found another in the house an hour ago. My sister made it only last week. Damn me if I didn't drop it in the fire – by mistake, of course!'

'The one here doesn't over provide for you either, sir. And – co-incidentally – we had an accident here also.'

'Champion, Quid! My sister is intestate, then. I'll get the lot!'

'Whatever you say, Commander – Mr Squeeze will see you now.'

Ray had heard the conversation through his open door, and checked the calendar to see if it was his birthday....

ELEVEN O'CLOCK FORENOON

Duncan sat in Lotte's chair, checking recently prepared mortgage papers, hand-written with meticulous care. Lotte stood smoothly to attention at his side, watching her senior making corrections, additions, deletions – and his usual quota of mistakes.

'Now, that's better, my dear,' smiled Duncan smugly. 'Get it typed and keep a copy as a style for your future guidance. These corrections are for your benefit – get it right from the start and you'll keep getting it right, that's what I say.'

'But you've made it wrong, Mr Smile.'

Lotte put her hand on Duncan's shoulder and leaned over, pointing her needle-sharp pencil at each of three blatant errors in Duncan's corrections. Duncan hardly saw the pencil – Lotte's long dark hair was tickling his cheek and his hearing was tuned to the rustle of her satin blouse.

'You're quite right, Lotte. I have no excuse to offer but the rotten night I've just had. Hardly got a wink. Just can't concentrate.'

Duncan reached for his pill-bottle, took a small pink capsule, swallowed with a grimace as if in pain, and excused himself. At the door, Duncan turned, composed himself and spoke authoritatively …

'This is the kind of thing which proves the value of consultation. You might not have been so certain that you were right unless I had made it easy for you to see that you were.'

Duncan liked the last word whether anyone, himself included, knew what he meant.

'Silly bat,' muttered Lotte, freshening her neck with spray-scent.

LUNCHTIME

Jerry left at 12.30 to lunch with Mr Squeers of the Building Society. A ruddy bore, Mr Squeers, but quite an ample provider of lunch. The rendezvous was the Cocktail Lounge of the Queen's Hotel – formerly a plush traditional establishment on the seafront, but now becoming a bit plasticy and yielding to the economic advantages of welcoming bus parties. One of such from the Midlands had just disgorged itself as Jerry arrived to a cacophony of strange accents, each expressing relief on sniffing the sea breezes after five or more hours cooped up in the coach. The bus-people divided in the foyer, some for the bar, but most for the loo. Jerry quickened his step to beat the new arrivals aiming for the bar, and got there just in time. Bert Squeers was already there, glass in hand, propped on a bar stool like a puppet on a stick, his shoes barely reaching the chrome foot-rail. Jerry staked his claim to the adjacent bar stool, and ordered his drink which, to his relief, promptly arrived. All in the nick of time, as it happens, because the bar was already filling up with coach-persons all dying of thirst, jostling for service.

After clearing the conversation from among of the usual claptrap –
'How's business?'
'Houses selling well?'
'Any loans?'
'Weather better … etc … etc …?' – Mr Squeers introduced a cheerier and more personal note into the chat – 'My wife's left me.'

Jerry was stricken with silent shock. Bert was not only a pillar of the building of marital solidarity, but also enjoyed the reputation of being a 'private person'.

'Oh how dreadful, Bert – I am both appalled and sorry,' was Jerry's diplomatic response.

It is expected that one should look shocked in such circumstances, and Jerry was well trained in showing the right face, whatever the circumstances. Deep down, he felt no surprise at all.

'Don't be, Jerry,' the wee man continued. 'I'm looking on this as something of a celebration drink – in fact, I've been celebrating since half past eleven!'

Right enough, thought Jerry, I've never seen the wee man so cheery – and slurring his speech more than a shade.

'She's a big woman, you know, and I've been bossed stupid for thirty years. Last night, I'd had enough and then some, and told her straight. She said she wasn't going to stay and have her authority challenged, packed her bags and left in a taxi, tout suite. In truth, Jerry, I feel nothing but relief.'

For once, Jerry was speechless. He needn't have worried, since his companion chattered on-

'Half seven, she left. She wouldn't have been at the end of the road when I was off to the Bowling Green. Had a great time. Didn't even need to be back by ten o'clock, or even sober for that matter. I watched my first ever late T.V. film with my feet up and a jolly good night-cap, sang loudly going upstairs at half past one in the morning, had a piping hot bath – right up to the top, not her bloody three inches 'for economy' – and slept like a log without any nagging or yards of stained corsets draped over my suit. It was heaven – same again please!'

His closing remark to the barman.

Bert's confidential disclosures were made easier by the throng and hubbub of the now packed lounge. What the wee man did not notice was a recent arrival, pushing through the crowd towards the bar-counter. An extremely big person with an extremely nasty expression and hands like hams. Indeed, Bert didn't know a thing, nor did the warmth inside him subside, till the creature was right beside him, grinning grotesquely.

'I couldn't leave you on your own, Bertram,' said Mrs Squeers, with a forced poshness never heard outside Troon. 'You need me to look after you, and I've come to do just that. Now, my dear, come along then.'

Bert hiccoughed audibly.

'Yes, my sweet,' said the wee man.

Squashing her husband against her with a massive arm, Mrs Squeers escorted him away, leaving Jerry next the vacant stool.

'Same again,' to the barman.

'That'll be £18.50, please – your friend hadn't got the length of producing his wallet.'

'Bloody hell,' muttered Jerry, producing a £20 note. 'Small price to pay just to witness a happy re-union, poor sod!'

He drank up, and went back to work without having eaten a morsel.

AFTERNOON

After their assortment of disturbed nights, bleary eyes had a harder than usual job to strain their peering through dirty windows into the grey gloom of the drizzle outside, wondering all the while how the weather could ever pick up in time for Wednesday's annual sporting highlight. Ray had gone home early, to escape Mrs Gow's wrath – or, hopefully so. Jerry, after his non-lunch tipped the contents of his full ashtray into the polythene lining specially inserted in his wastebasket only. The cleaners, though anything but fastidious, had long since got fed up with the half-inch of ash which formerly adorned the carpet when emptying the thing.

Lighting another fag, Jerry swung his rolled umbrella at paper balls as if with a short iron, spraying the missiles as far to the right and left as he usually did with the real thing. Concentrating hard this time, left hand gripping with determination, weight over the left foot and with firm wrists, intent to keep the ruddy thing on line, Jerry wound himself into a controlled backswing but, breaking all the boffins' rules in the process, whooshed into the ball with venom. Missing it topside, he clipped the striplight overhead with his follow-through. The resultant explosion was deafening, and, with only a short pause, Zoë and Miss Nockersby opened his door gingerly, and squinted round the gap expecting a messy suicide and blood-strewn walls. Jerry was sitting on the floor, grinning from ear to ear, his greying hair sparkling with glass fragments as if wearing a diamond tiara.

'You all right, Mr Quid?' enquired the latter.

'Never been better, Miss Nockersby!' quavered Jerry, obviously shaken.

'Oh well,' chipped in Zoë, 'You'll be able to see Mrs Gow – she's come to enquire when Mr Squeeze's funeral is, and Mr Smile refuses to see her.'

'Give me a minute to shake off the glass, m'dear, then show Mrs Gow in, please.'

Jerry was about to light another fag when he noticed that the one he had been smoking had fallen into his breast pocket and had burned itself through. Replacing the packet in his jacket, and muttering something unlikely about giving up the filthy habit, Jerry found himself facing Mrs Gow, all in black and with a veil covering her face – which made her decidedly easier to look at.

Raising a lace-edged handkerchief to her reddened nose, Mrs Gow sat down with a solemnity equal to *her* understanding of the occasion.

'I'm so sorry, Mr Quid, really I am. Mr Squeeze and I had many a harsh word, but in truth I thought he was a lovely man.'

Jerry winced at the description.

'You must be grief stricken, you and Mr Smile,' the lady sobbed on, 'Did most of the work here, Mr Squeeze did – or so he said – oh, it's a tragedy, and him so young too...'

Jerry felt compelled to interrupt.

'Now, Mrs Gow, don't you upset yourself – there's obviously been a misunderstanding. It's not *our* Mr Squeeze who has died. It is his... his grandfather – yes, that's right, *his grandfather* – yes, that's who it is that has died!'

Jerry felt proud of his masterly handling of a tricky situation.

'HIS GRANDFATHER, is it!' Mrs Gow shouted, lifting the veil off her face, which screwed up like a grotesque rubber walnut. 'HIS GRANDFATHER!' she repeated, contorting violently, 'And I sent ten pounds-worth of flowers to his home and the bastard's not dead – by God, Quid, I'll be expecting compensation. Mark my words, I'll see to it that I get bloody compensation. Yes, that's what I'll get, and no bloody messing, you'll see!'

The lady got up and swept out the door without turning and swerved downstairs with her shrill screech echoing off the tiled walls.

'His GRANDFATHER, indeed, his GRANDFATHER!'

By 4.30 p.m. only the hard-working staff were left in the office. Messrs. Quid and Squeeze, hard on Duncan's heels, each had to leave early 'on business'. In truth, each was rapt in anticipation of the Golf Outing, and, by six o'clock, three car boots were suitably filled with bag, clubs, shoes, waterproofs and the usual gadgetry of the links. Tuesday evening dragged on interminably, like the few long hours before the bells announce the arrival of a New Year. Each, in his own way, was gasping for the arrival of the Big Day.

So was Miss Bottoms – she was to use her Wednesday off (weather permitting) displaying her new miniscule bikini and its voluminous contents – at a beach party with her new boyfriend. Duncan would rather be going to the beach party too, but his wife wouldn't let him – nor would Miss Bottoms!

WEDNESDAY THE EIGHTEENTH

It has to be admitted that the British summer has precious little of the equatorial about it, save in the Monsoon Season of the latter. Especially so in northern Britain, where Ian McCaskill and Bill Giles decree that transatlantic clouds head north-east at the Irish Sea so to allow Scotland and upper England wholesome rain and lush verdure, whilst condemning those poor folks living south of Wigan to the torture of blue skies, drought and tanned bodies – especially in the Home Counties, for which locale is reserved the best of United Kingdom temperatures – and the best of much else besides, courtesy of whatever is the government of the day.

This Scottish summer has been its usual windy, showery self, with just about enough sun and warmth to lower the suicide statistics and to raise the spirits and colour the gardens. To the considerable joy of some thirty local lawyers, today is quite extraordinarily pleasant – flat calm, hot early morning sun, and clouds as absent as priests at a Temperance meeting. The six a.m. birdcall and the sound of a tortoise rustling through last year's dead leaves comprised the only noises necessary to waken Jerry – indeed, the tortoise could probably have managed on its own. Never has Jerry jumped out of bed so enthusiastically for his work, and the singing beneath the lukewarm shower had his wife Anne unwillingly on her feet. For her, this would indeed be the longest day – and God knows what would be coming home at the end of it all! However, she sportingly shared Jerry's undisguised joy, and served up a quite sumptuous 7a.m. breakfast on the terrace, with a pot of steaming coffee for the second and third cups.

With a gentle kiss and a fond farewell, as if going abroad on active military service, Jerry left Anne at the gate and drove off, waving.

Everything happened somewhat differently chez Squeeze. Marjory had to shake Ray violently to semi-consciousness at 8.15 a.m., and by the time the bleary-eyed lawyer had slurped his breakfast in bed, he dozed off again and was yanked bodily to the floor at twenty-five to nine. In only ten minutes, Ray was steering the Rover out the driveway, clipping the gatepost with his nearside en route. His clothes looked as if shovelled on by a navvy, and the odd button which was done up was in the wrong hole. His crumpled tie and jacket lay on the floor beneath the glove-locker, ready for use in the Clubhouse Lounge. Switching on the car radio, his ears were regaled by a screeching Moira Anderson, and a quick change of channel brought a curse as Terry Wogan modestly swaggered his dexterity with the English language as only the non-English are capable. For safety, Ray pushed his tape-button and tunelessly sang along with the Seven Dwarfs from the sound-track of the Disney masterpiece, courtesy of his children, the only ones who could coax his wallet into daylight, a feat of no mean accomplishment, be assured. Halfway to the golf course, Ray started to think about women. For some unimaginable reason Ray found golf courses to be sexually exciting. It takes all sorts.

Duncan got up at 7.15 a.m., bathed, dressed and went straight into the dining room, sat down in his personal carver chair and applied his right slippered foot to the floor-button concealed beneath the carpet, summoning service. He'd probably have shouted to Doreen after a few seconds to 'get a bloody move on', but his eye caught sight of a half full (or half empty) bottle of red wine on the melamine sideboard – neglected in favour of a liqueur the previous evening – and ruminatively sank the lot in four hurried glassfuls. Just as he had replaced the glass in the drinks-cupboard, having 'cleaned' it with the tail of his shirt, the harassed Doreen appeared with a salver of devilled kidneys, bacon, mushrooms, sausages and fried potatoes, and proceeded to serve the considerable meal on to a pre-heated plate. Duncan polished the cutlery with his napkin, then polished off the entire contents of the plate, cleaning the moisture left with a third slice of fresh-buttered bread.

'Not bad, Doreen,' said Duncan, licking the grease off his lips.

By God, he must be in a good mood to pay such an elegant tribute. Doreen had stood smartly to attention at his side throughout the ritual breakfast, apron still on, and shaking nervously in case the master had further needs. On hearing her husband's appreciative remark, Doreen's hands stopped shaking, and she summoned the bravery to ask for five pounds to do some shopping.

'Certainly, my dear!' smiled Duncan, as he handed over his purse. 'Help yourself!'

Doreen nearly collapsed, but steadied herself on a chairback, peeled out the desired fiver, returned the purse, bowed, and wished her husband luck. Duncan felt good. Must try to be kind more often, he thought.

As he drove to the golf course, Duncan's good humour turned to his usual aggression at the wheel, and he covered the fifteen-mile journey in twelve minutes with a harrowing quota of near misses.

Jerry had been in the clubhouse for forty minutes when Duncan entered, and for a good hour by the time that Ray attracted some good-humoured attention by adorning the lounge with one black shoe, and one tan. He blushed somewhat when his minor sartorial disarray was drawn to his attention, but boldly announced that he was prepared to be judged on golfing merit, not on style of dress. After all, it is a golf match, not a fashion show.

Coffee cups drained, and only the early brandy-swillers left, the exodus to the changing rooms got under way. The day proper was about to start, and the weather remained totally perfect. Duncan was afflicted with wind and hiccoughs – both with identifiable cause – and not even the animated chat of the enthusiasts could disguise the effects of the former of these. Jerry was last in, having stopped at the notice board on which was posted the names of the entire legal party. Something to do with the Licensing Regulations. The pairings were also listed, and this is how the relevant sections read:-

FACULTY of SOLICITORS
Party – Wednesday – 18 June

Harry Amos	Ian Sook	Norman Chalmers
George Crudd	Peter Crudd	Neil Crudd
Gibson Macdonald	Farquhar Pickforth	Jerome L. Quid
Arthur J. Crowe	William L. Sewell	James Slash
Duncan Smile	Raymond Squeeze	Herbie Gilmour

Sheriffs Clapp and Marbles and Dean of Faculty Ben Doon
Sundry other threesomes –
And George S. Dale (Non-playing)

Jerry whistled through his teeth. Farquhar he could tolerate, just, but Gibson Macdonald was a real swine. Damn fool who arranged the pairings, or triplings. Harry Amos and his playing partners were putting out for three crisp sixes at the fourth (two of them missed) as Jerry laced up his golf shoes, whilst at the third, all three Crudd brothers were wondering by what quirk of fate a random draw of names had found them in each other's company. That the Crudds were together was not without risks. All right, so no one else had to play with any of them – but who would believe it if any of them came in with the winning card? Jerry's trio were comfortably behind them and at least the Crudds were sober at this time of day, though distinctly hungover.

The first groups out played unapologetic rubbish. It is hard to imagine what it was that they had been looking forward to! The real golf, comparatively speaking, came nearer mid-morning, by when all thirty-three swingers were at various stages of the course.

Jerry was in a greenside bunker at the sixth in two, Farquhar just short in three. Gibson Macdonald, on the green in two, was behind whins having a jimmy. He didn't take his eyes off either of the other two, however. So intent was he to ensure that his playing partners took no advantage of his temporary inconvenience (or 'convenience'), Gibson returned to the green, pulling up his zip, with his trousers soaking from crotch to knees. No one passed any comment, though a zoomed close-up of either Farquhar or Jerry would have detected the hint of a smile. Gibson was not a nice person when riled, or even otherwise for the most part.

Farquhar laid his fourth stiff for a five, and winked to Jerry as he retrieved his ball from the cup. Jerry took four to get out of the bunker, then lifted up. Left to his birdie chance, Gibson took an interminable time to line up his shot from every conceivable angle, and then stood motionless above his ball as the skylarks gave it laldy overhead.

'Switch off the birds for Mr Macdonald!' quipped Jerry.

Macdonald stood back from his ball theatrically and frowned sourly.

'Shut up, will you, while I'm putting!' glowered the gent.

Silence restored, the skylarks aside, Gibson retook his stance. Halfway through his measured backstroke, a bellow hollered from a hundred yards back.

'GET A BLOODY MOVE ON, YOU LOT!'

It was Jim Slash, clad in yellow from head to foot, like a giant canary, but without the grace of a cormorant.

Gibson couldn't hold back. His climactic putt had passed its point of no return and, charged up and bursting, hit the ball too hard so that it glided across the green, undulating and twisting hither and thither. As its energies diminished and came near to resting six yards past the hole, the spent ball teetered atop a shaven hard-baked mound, then picked up speed again as it scurried downhill and plopped into the burn which had been waiting for it all the time.

Macdonald was a study, what with purple anger darkening his face against his mane of white hair, and the state of his trousers! Jerry lifted his bag and headed for the seventh tee. To have repeated Macdonald's language in this narrative would have it banned from publication, so what followed is left to the readers' imagination. Suffice to say that a couple of unavailing attempts to play his ball from the burn completely saturated Macdonald's entire frontispiece so that his involuntary dribbles of a few moments earlier paled into nothingness in comparison with his comprehensive self-inflicted hose-down.

Two matches back, Ray had started with four fours, Duncan with a five and three sixes, and Herbie with a three and three fives. There's more than one way to skin a cat, or play a golf course. The fifth was five hundred and twenty five yards long, playing shorter on account of the heat, which was dispelling very quickly the after-effects of the previous week's wet weather, one of the several merits of a seaside links course.

Ray clattered a driver some two hundred and eighty yards, mid-fairway. Herbie was straight, but some seventy yards shorter. Duncan sliced a three-wood as nearly as is geometrically possible at right angles to its intended path, clearing the stone dyke which formed the landward boundary of the course, and into the path of a goods train on the line over the wall. With a sharp crack which could be heard above the rumble of the diesel engine, the ball sailed back as near as dammit from whence it had been propelled, and came to its gashed rest on a perfect fairway lie some fifty yards forward of the tee.

'Jammy bastard,' said Ray, becoming irritated with Duncan's aberrations. 'Don't even get properly punished for the worst tripe you play. Hell, man, a straight fifty yard drive is good by your standards; it's the way you get there that's getting up my bloody nose!'

'Nonsense!' replied Duncan, good-naturedly. 'I do that every year at this hole.'

He probably did.

A three-wood saw Ray just short and slightly left. Herbie's next two shots left his ball six inches from the flagstick. Three ungainly swipes had Duncan in whins, a bunker and down a rabbit-hole respectively. With a free drop from the last of these, he was in with a chance of his fourth successive six, but actually took eight.

For Ray's third, which was lying bare, he had to negotiate a deep bunker which yawned invitingly between him and the flag, which waved gently but mockingly.

'What is it to be then, mate?' enquired Duncan. 'Is it to be a top into the bunker, or one of your nice shanks across the green and into the pretty bushes?'

'Bugger off!' snapped Ray. Having scored well thus far, he was settling into serious vein.

After the usual preliminaries, and a few of his individual fol-de-rols for good measure, Ray slowly lifted his wedge with textbook precision, eye glued to the ball, and, with the minutest pause at the top of his swing, eased the club gently but firmly into the ball as his weight moved graciously on to the sole of his left foot. The club pressed the ball downwards and forwards, and its loft did the rest. Up and up, as if in slow motion, the ball sailed easily over the bunker, its backspin whistling like a top. When its forward thrust was spent, the ball fell out of the blue sky and plopped softly on the waiting green six inches beyond the hole, writhed momentarily in spin, then crawled back just enough to disappear, to keep company with the base of the flagstick.

Beaming with unrestrained joy, Ray punched the air in triumph, and accepted the outstretched congratulatory hands of his companions.

'Eagle three – Albatross two with my stroke – five points. Now let's hear no more of all this shanking nonsense!'

Four holes and five shanks later, Ray reached the turn in 43, and felt sick. Bloody hell, even Herbie had managed out in 44. Duncan took 56 to reach the same distance and remained cheery, which only angered Ray the more.

'WHERE'S GEORGE DALE?' yelled Ray, as he hurled his golf bag on to the tenth tee

THE TENT

George Dale, mid seventies, semi-retired, five feet one inch and a good sixteen stones plus, didn't play golf. His annual presence at the Golf Outing had, however, been an institution ever since most of the regular participants could remember. Every year, whatever the weather, George sat atop a grassy mound behind the green at the short tenth. The mound was a good twenty feet above the putting surface, and commanded an excellent view over the entire tenth hole and much else of the course besides, not to mention the clubhouse clock. George walked his plus-foured legs with the aid of a stick and, for the last few years, had required help to reach his perch. He could have probably made it on his own, but George carried with him to the mound a rather special consignment. And there was never any shortage of volunteers to help George with his burden. George was affectionately known as 'The Tent' – short for Refreshment Tent in the idiom of the big sponsored tournaments, and the competitors took time out after playing the tenth hole to sample the miscellany of beers, wines and spirits which George donated annually as his contribution to the day's good humour.

'Hurry up and get the tenth over,' snarled Ray. 'And here's hoping those Crudd bastards haven't drunk the lot'.

Duncan had finished the ninth in his first four of the day by dint of sinking a long iron, and was to tee off first at the tenth. Ray and Herbie never saw Duncan's shot – their eyes were homed in on George Dale's refreshment tent on the mound just 150 yards away. So they missed

Duncan's club selection – a clumsily senseless two-iron. All Duncan's playing partners heard was the crack of club on ball, it, for once, in the middle of what is referred to as the sweet-spot. The ball shot like the bullet from a rifle dead on line for the crouching George Dale, who was responding to a request from James Slash for a second double brandy. Halfway from the tee, Duncan's ball arced upwards and seemed to take predetermined aim for George's right hand which had removed a fresh bottle from one of two crates. No one heard any cry of 'Fore!'

Duncan, Ray and Herbie just took on a resigned look, and three jaws dropped despairingly as ball and bottle connected, the latter smashed to pieces and the former rebounding on the the green and disappearing into the cup, leaving the flag and everyone else limp with astonishment.

'Good God Almighty!' snarled Ray. 'That'll cost you! Hole in one indeed – but you're supposed to buy the drinks, not smash them!'

Duncan broke into uncontrolled laughter and nearly choked on his ever-excited dentures. Ray and Herbie holed out in commendable threes, whilst Duncan swaggered in the clamour of invisible and inaudible applause, taking bows to left and right and raising his worn cap as he dreamed on to the eleventh tee.

Whilst he was doing so, Ray and Herbie raced up the mound behind the tenth to grab their drinks from where George was plucking glass fragments from his thorn-proofs, smelling like a pub and smiling warmly. No one had bothered to replace the tenth flag, which swung on its point of balance on the greenside, overhanging a bunker. Some thumping doubles consumed, Ray and Herbie re-joined Duncan on the eleventh tee, having threaded the winding blaes path with difficulty and good humour, feeling inwardly warm to match the summer temperature.

Two holes beyond was the lucky thirteenth – twice across the burn which snaked its way across the links, Jerry and Gibson had an arm around each other's shoulders as they staggered good-naturedly to where their tee-shots lay two inches apart from each other.

'That's what I call target golf, Gibbie,' slurred Jerry. 'Your shot first, I think.'

'Not at all, old boy, after you.' Bowing gracefully, Jerry dropped his clubs and his fag and yanked out a three iron unsteadily. As he commenced his address, Jerry's head began to swim and he found himself looking down at four balls and holding two clubs.

'Which of these bloody balls do I hit?' muttered Jerry to himself. Believing that to get it over quickly was his preferred option, Jerry swung with all the might he could muster, and all four balls disappeared into the sun. Farquhar, whose behaviour at George's watering hole had been somewhat more judicious, saw the flight of both balls, sailing as if in formation and both hitting mid-green and drawing up to where all three Crudd brothers were lying to each other about the number of strokes in which each had holed out.

'I didn't know you did trick-shots, Jerry,' smiled Macdonald. 'And thanks, pal, for putting my drive on to the green!'

Jerry was uneasy about the way the ground kept going up and down, and wondered how he'd manage to face the lunchtime drinks.

He needn't have worried.

At the clubhouse, the early starters who had raced round the course with no one in front to delay them, had doctored their scorecards, changed in the locker-room and repaired to the bar. By the time the Crudds joined Amos Book and Chalmers, poor Chalmers was clearly stoned – an unhappy state with lunch awaiting the arrival of the final trio, an hour or so away. Of course, Norman carried his own flask with him as well as having participated fully at George Dale's 'Tent'. He had managed a 4 at the first, a 5 at the second and a 6 at the third. Whether the progression to a 22 at the eighteenth materialised was impossible to determine from examination of his scorecard, illegible and saturated in whisky. By 12.30, Norman was in a taxi on his way home, unfed and anything but well. Lucky Mrs Chalmers!

A few mouthfuls of clean water out the burn revived Jerry who played quite well for the rest of the round. The old pals' act with Macdonald didn't extend beyond the fifteenth, by which time both had sobered up, and Gibson had blown his top at an accusation of cheating.

'Cheating my arse!' snapped Macdonald. 'That was a practice swing.'

'Was it hell!' thundered Jerry. 'D'you think I'm bloody blind?'

'You mind your language, rat-face,' retorted the white hair, face reddening.

Jerry didn't reply, got his head down and finished with three par fours. This gave him 28 points, creditable enough, but unlikely to see him garlanded in the winner's enclosure. That skunk Macdonald had only 22, and Farquhar had 26, so Jerry glowed just a wee bit, and retired to the clubhouse bar and sat with Farquhar as far away as possible from the older of his two morning companions, drawing from his cold drink in huge gulps, and from his fag with equal enthusiasm.

Half an hour later Ray (31 points) and Duncan (11) joined Jerry after the obligatory visit to the bar, having left Herbie Gilmour there in animated conversation with the barmaid.

Ian Sook was his usual puffed up self, voice booming through his scruffy ginger and grey beard above the hubbub of the now full bar.

'So I just told Sheriff Clapp straight,' Ian bellowed, 'get off my back or you'll be back on your paper-round! "Please accept my apology Mr Sook," the Sheriff replied. "I accept that I may have exceeded my authority" MAY have? I replied. The poor bugger was looking quite upset, so I didn't insist that he should crawl, as had been my first intention – but these laddies need to be kept in their place. You realise of course, chaps, that I do this for all of us. If you court chaps get a smooth passage, it's because I keep these Sheriff laddies in check. Any of them coming for lunch?'

Sheriff Clapp had, in fact, arrived ten minutes earlier, and, whilst partially concentrating on Duncan's fawning and superfluous words of welcome, couldn't help overhearing much of the Sook boor's resonances. Asking to be excused from Duncan, the Sheriff threaded through the throng and loomed before Sook, whose eyes noticeably bulged in surprise inside the over-sized lenses of his tinted designer spectacles.

'We were just talking about you, Sheriff, smarmed Ian on the basis that attack would be more remedial than defence.

'So I heard, Mr Sook – I'm very flattered that I should warrant a mention from such a senior member of Faculty. You'll be remembering that you have a trial before me tomorrow – do try and be gentle with me.'

Ian blushed, and his audience laughed heartily and aimed toward the dining room, leaving scruffy-beard on his own, like a preacher in an empty church.

Lunch was a noisy affair, hearts beating fast in anticipation of the afternoon foursomes. Ray, excited not only by the golf but also by four large gins, found the waitresses well worth some scintillating chatting-up and before even finishing his main course, had arranged to meet at least two of them behind the greenkeepers' sheds. Grimacing something about coming prepared, his exact words were lost in a mixture of slurring and slavered pathos. It should be said, however, that Ray was all chat, and none too scintillating at that. However, he had good cause to feel tremblingly embarrassed as he stood on the first tee in the afternoon, and when he espied a bare female arm beckoning towards him from the very area which he had suggested. He had his playing partners out of breath as he raced them through the first hole to the safety of the copse which obscured the second tee from the sight of the frustrated lady. He didn't feel safe until he reached the third green, at which distance the clubhouse looked not much bigger than a matchbox.

Ahead of Ray and Jerry, drawn to play together, a severely refreshed Neil Crudd and his partner Gibson Macdonald were embattled, quite literally. At the twelfth, Crudd crowned Macdonald with his putter for having missed a six-incher. Whilst silently complimenting Neil on his aim, the others in their foursome intervened and escorted the blooded Macdonald back to the clubhouse for treatment. Neil's golf bag, which Macdonald had kicked into a bunker, was found by the green staff the following morning. Neil, left on his own, decided to go for a swim, having already twice fallen into the burn. He forgot to take any of his clothes off before entering the sea, and only really sobered up when he swallowed some soiled toilet paper, borne on the tide from a nearby sewage-pipe.

Of all the afternoon participants, the Ray and Jerry partnership was the clear favourite, on handicap anyway. The ones otherwise to watch were afternoon only competitors, namely old Henderson Logan and Watty Wilson – principally Logan. Old Logan never lost a ball. His golfing trousers were specially designed with an internal pouch for holding balls of matching make and number, and an escape-hole through which he could expel a fresh one via his trouser-leg, if finding himself in heavy rough or in one of the many whin-bushes. His familiar call of 'It's all right boys, I've found it!' echoed just about every second hole, and there he'd be, lying in the clear no matter into what impossible location he had whacked the thing. How on earth the old fool could be bothered was beyond the imagination of most people, but for as long as he never actually won, his barely disguised secret remained diplomatically un-blown.

Ian Sook was unusually subdued, not that his golf was much worse than that of his three inept companions, but he hadn't much to say to anyone of his own age anyway, preferring to speak down to those whom he considered to be his juniors or inferiors. In any event, Ian and his fellow competitors were invariably at issue one way or another and, chastened a little bit by his lunch time encounter with Sheriff Clapp, he was saving his voice until the speech making at the prizegiving, when his aptitude for tasteless interruptions would have greater scope.

David Crudd had mishit about every second shot over the first nine holes. Eighty yards from the tenth green (George Dale and his refreshment tent did not make a practice of attending the afternoon session) David enquired around

'What should I do with this one – what club do you suggest?'

'Just hit the ------ thing, you clown!' bellowed his long-suffering partner.

This authoritative instruction was acted on with due immediacy, and David quickly hooked a three, yes a three iron, miles left straight through a picture window in the Clubhouse lounge-bar, spraying a be-monocled gent with glass fragments and, more importantly obliging the gent to drop his brandy.

'God dammit!' thundered the gent. 'These bloody visitors should be banned. Peasants the lot of them. Shouldn't be allowed within miles of here.'

'Easy, Fingal,' calmed his drinking companion, anxious for his friend's blood pressure. 'We'd have to pay a bonny subscription without visitors' green-fees.'

'Piffle!' responded the monocle. 'We always managed in the old days. If you're that bloody much in their favour at least buy me another drink, and make it a very large one.'

When his fresh drink arrived, Fingal filtered the glass-fragmented dregs of his spilled drink through a handkerchief into the new glass. This done, and just about to say 'Cheers', the door of the oaken lounge swung open and David Crudd reeled in, spiked shoes, golfbag and all, seemingly prepared to play his next shot out through the broken window.

Fingal dropped his new brandy in utter astonishment.

'Get the hell out of here, you swine!' screamed the gent. 'Get me the Captain. Get the police; get anyone – but get rid of THAT!!' pointing at David.

'Even if I can't play it from here then,' slurred David, 'may I please have my ball back?'

Fingal fainted and was brought round, eventually, with more brandy.

Such was the intensity of the gladiators' concentration on other things, there was no notice taken that the morning's heat-haze over the sea had turned purplish-black. The sun was still shining and the heat was still rising, but all the afternoon, the heaviness of the darkening western sky was creeping its way towards the shore. It took a frightening burst of thunder to draw attention to this particularly alarming of nature's phenomena, and, literally in a flash of blinding silver light against the new black sky, the heavens opened. Raindrops the size of garden peas fell as if out of clear overhead skies, then positively cascaded in a downpour of Biblical proportions. As the clouds covered the sun, a fierce wind sprung up and the on-course hostilities came to an abrupt halt. As more lightning flashed in a crescendo of rain and thunderclaps, everyone ran for the shelter of the Clubhouse, leaving balls in situ, even those only inches from the flagstick.

Ray stopped in the locker-room just long enough to grab his day-clothes then headed for home before his waitress-friends confronted him about the possibility of an evening tryst. He had, as it happens, won the Sheriff Clapp Trophy for his morning's performance, about which he remembered when presented with it by Duncan in the Office the following day.

By the time that all the others were safe in the clubhouse, there was a sober silence as each took in the terror of the electric storm from the picture windows, grateful for their very lives.

Ian Sook, himself, was quiet, and any conversation was in whispers as if in reverential presence of the Almighty. Soft drinks, rather than further risks, were taken, and the lawyers' behaviour was so courteous and restrained that even Fingal and his friend, the former in a state of alcoholic emotionalism at 5 p.m., wished them well and expressed a tearful hope that they'd all return next year.

FIVESKIN – AND BETTY

Ray flicked a gooey globule of marmalade off his tie and wiped his right forefinger on his trouser leg. Dialling Miss Bottoms for black coffee, his finger discovered where the globule had splodged, and Ray repeated the process, this time pushing the marmalade through the dial of the phone; then sneezing vociferously and messily, he HAD to go to the gents for a toilet tissue to clean up the spattered trading accounts of the Fiveskin Trading Group, for whose assets a prospective purchaser was about to arrive.

Mr Fiveskin – who always expected a cheery reaction when referring to his father as 'Old Foreskin' – had left Ray to negotiate, or milk, or salvage as much out of the commercial wreckage as could be procured. It almost seemed on purpose that Ray's copy set of accounts was faint to the point of illegibility – not least that bit intended to demonstrate the name and address of the auditors. Ray's clumsy repair-work with tissue on the multicoloured-sprayed areas did nothing to improve the clarity of the print, and when Messrs Morris and MacPherson were shown in, Ray's smile was both artificial and nervous.

Holding out a pale bony hand, the former of the two gents announced himself –

'Lawrence Morris of International Toys Tobacco and Tinwear.'

Ray took his hand unenthustically and signalled him towards the seat next to where MacPherson had lowered his bulk warily. Before accepting Ray's invitation, Mr Morris aimed his skeletal forefinger at his colleague's neck and introduced Mr Ivor MacPherson, a red-haired barrel of a man with eyes like black buttons.

'Mr MacPherson is my accountant, Mr Squeeze.'

With both men seated, Ivor spoke. 'We have come to talk money, Mr Squeeze. We know that Fiveskin is in big trouble and that we'd be doing him a favour just to relieve him of his obligations. However, fair's fair – there may be outlets for us through his connections, so we're prepared to be reasonable. How's about a shufty at the trading figures, then?'

'Certainly, Mr MacPherson. You'll have to forgive the quality of the print, though. Our photocopier is on the blink, and the only carbon copies my clients gave me were mauled by my dog last night and haven't responded too well to ironing.'

Ray smiled as if to enquire whether there was the remotest chance his story might be believed. He didn't, after all, have a dog.

'Thought there'd be something of the sort, Mr Squeeze – so we got our own set of accounts from the Companies Registration Office, and we'll use our set, if you don't mind. I can see, even upside down, lousy print and all, that your lot is three years old.'

'Be assured, gentlemen,' Ray blushed, 'There was positively no intent to deceive you into believing otherwise.'

'It wouldn't have worked if you had, Mr Squeeze. Mr Morris and I didn't come up the river on skis. Now then, I see Fiveskin made last year a gross profit of £54,000 and a net profit of £500 only.'

'It would have been a net profit of nearer £20,000 hadn't it been for bank overdraft interest.'

'That's Fiveskin's hard lines, sir. It's a wonder we're not talking to a liquidator, or receiver – does the bank have a charge?'

'Thought you'd have known that from your research,' replied Ray sardonically.

'We do,' said MacPherson. 'Just wondered if YOU did.'

Ray was getting angry. He didn't like any kind of sarcasm, except his own, at which he excelled.

'Look,' he snapped. 'I am an agent with instructions to sell – are you interested on buying, or are we wasting each other's time? If you want to buy, name your price. You have obviously come here well equipped with all the relevant gen and with a specific purpose – now spill, or get going. I'm a busy man.'

Mr Morris stirred himself from his huddled silence and joined in the conversation – 'Keep calm, Mr Squeeze. Mr MacPherson may not be a candidate for the Diplomatic Corps, but he is a very good accountant. He just wishes you to know the need to be realistic when it comes to the financial aspects of any deal to be done.'

'Name your price or get going,' yawned Ray. 'I have another engagement in five minutes.'

Ray allowed himself a glance out the window to check the weather. His quarter-final tie at the Club was due to tee off in half an hour, and he wasn't going to let squirts like Morris and MacPherson have him disqualified for want of punctuality.

'£20,000,' chorused the duo.

'Get your lawyers to put that in writing and there's a deal,' said Ray rising to his feet and edging towards the door. Ignoring the handshakes proffered by Messrs M & M as they made to leave, Ray slammed the door behind them. He then retrieved Fiveskin's written instruction from the filing cabinet and smiled as he re-read 'try to get me off the hook for £5,000.'

Ray tore up the note, chucked the pieces into his wastebucket and sloped off to the golf course, chuckling.

As he entered the clubhouse, the lawyer thought again about Fiveskin's instruction. Did 'Mr Foreskin's son' want to receive £5,000 – or was he prepared to PAY £5,000 just to get shot of a bad lot? C'est la guerre! One way or the other should be good for a bloody huge fee, I'd think!

Ray's smile vanished as his tee-shot at the first hole sailed out of bounds on to the foreshore.

'Bugger it,' he snapped. 'Nothing ever goes right these days!'

When on the golf course, all else, however recently occurred, does not exist.

Duncan Smile scanned his watch and rubbed his eyes. 'Eleven o'clock only,' he muttered, flopping into his squishy chair with a huge yawn. He looked round the room counting the cobwebs, bit a couple of nails from his left hand, pared the rough edges with a rusty penknife and swivelled round towards the window. Seagull droppings weaved a jolly embroidery of patterns on the glass. Turning his head from side to side and up and down, Duncan tried to make out pictures and designs – yawning all the while like a bored kitten looking for a leaf to chase.

Having dealt with both letters in his morning mail, and being too early for lunch, Duncan considered that his indolence would be less noticeable if he got out of the office 'on business'. But, where to go? 'I've got it!' he assured himself, picked up his anorak from the floor and on leaving shouted to Mrs Mulcaster at Reception.

'I have a meeting in town at 11.30. Probably be back just after lunch.'

When, as today, Duncan suffered from total ennui, his solution was to go and look at new cars. Driving towards town, which boasted four main dealerships plus agencies and showrooms aplenty to absorb his interest in all things metallic and shiny, Duncan surveyed his own year-old saloon, its carpet littered with sweet papers and chip-bags, dog-ends and a miscellany of garments, and promised himself that he was en route, not just to look, but to buy. None of the lower end of the market stuff for Duncan, which ruled out some of the foreign muck and not a little of its home-grown equivalent. Nothing small, nothing too flashy, but something DIFFERENT, something to spell out to all and sundry that whilst he was in partnership he remained – nominally at least – the SENIOR partner. He parked in the multi-storey, electing to walk on his mission.

Duncan averted his eyes streetwards when passing the Rolls Royce/Bentley dealers. No point in looking at fillet steak if you plan to order rissoles. Waiting to cross a cobbled side street, Duncan spotted a new brightly-lit sign at its far end, and allowed curiosity to draw him nearer to read the wording of the sign. His pace quickened as he made out '**Customise your Car Ltd**'.

As he entered the premises, he found himself in a large warm carpeted office, heavy with the aroma of freshly made coffee. The panelled walls were decorated with framed portraits of 'Customers' Cars converted to order.' The girl behind the padded counter wore a delightfully out-of-fashion mini-skirt of dark blue tartan and a yellow polo-neck sweater swollen with bosoms.

Duncan breathed in sharply and ran the back of his hand over his glistening brow.

Can I help you, sir?' enquired the young lady

'Pardon?' enquired Duncan, taking in her huge blue eyes and immaculately made-up face.

'Can I help you, sir, I said,' smiled the girl, totally and not unhappily conscious of her impact on the possible customer.

'Oh yes, dear,' trying unsuccessfully to look unruffled, 'Do you have a male member?'

'I beg your pardon, sir,' frowned the young lady, whose soft features took on a markedly harder look, her eyes darkening a shade.

'A male assistant, I mean,' stuttered Duncan.

'You're not buying contraceptives, sir. Unless you are planning to say something offensive, you can speak freely to me. I am the owner of this company.'

'Oh, I see.' Duncan shuffled his feet and blew his nose. 'Well, I have a year old Granada. I find it functional, well engineered, roomy – but dull. I think it could do with a facelift – what can you suggest?'

'We don't get many people asking to have their Granadas doctored, but I'll phone our London end if you want. They do a lot of business for theatrical people – are you in show business, sir – or do you always walk about with your flies undone?'

As Duncan made a two-handed grab for his zip, a mountain of a man came through a door from the back-shop, took in the scene, and snapped.

'Do you want me to hang one on this geyser, Betty?'

Poor Mr Smile didn't wait to hear the girl's response, but ran for the door and all the way back to the multi-storey carpark. Only when in the safety of his car with all doors locked did Duncan stop shaking. He sat in silence for ten minutes till his heartbeat returned to normal, took a couple of tranquillisers, and drove very slowly back to the office. The Granada would do for a while yet, nothing wrong with it that a good clean wouldn't cure.

Jerry stuck his head round Duncan's door at 12.15

'I had coffee with the Chief Constable this morning. He says there's a flasher been reported in town. Got a good description too. I've often wondered what these people really look like!'

Duncan gulped, excused himself to leave for an early lunch and returned mid-afternoon wearing dark glasses. Within a week, his beard was quite bushy.

BREATHSTONE AND ROXANNE

Jerry lit a fag and sought inspiration from the spiral of blue smoke.

'It's all very well for you to say it goes without saying when you don't tell me what you're talking about.'

'All I said, Jerry, was that you should have gone to Sid's funeral,' replied Ray '– and that, surely, goes without saying. Blimey, old Sid was like a father to you.'

'Sid and I had an arrangement, mate. We agreed that since it was unlikely he'd come to my funeral I wasn't to go to his. Funerals aren't like weddings where you can go to each others, you know.'

Far from impressed by Jerry's seeming hard-heartedness, Ray nonetheless grasped the logic of his argument, and left his partner alone in the fug of his room. The rain fair stotted off the flat roof outside Jerry's window, leaving him with the comforting thought that only a madman would venture out to see his lawyer on such a day.

Five minutes later, that comfort was shattered by word that a Mr Breathstone was in the waiting room for his appointment.

'What bloody appointment?' muttered Jerry as he scanned his diary. Right enough, in Mrs Mulcaster's handwriting, the note showed '3.30 p.m. Cyril Breathstone'. God, she'd even spelled it correctly. Wonders never cease.

The bulbous-eyed Breathstone was shown in, smelling strongly of tonic water mixed with gin to the ratio of one part of the former and six of the latter. He enquired nervously if he may smoke, not that there was any shortage in the room of smoke, enough for two even, before Breathstone lit up. These preliminaries seen to, the client hung his saturated hat and coat on top of Jerry's new Burberry, and open the dialogue.

'Mr Quid, I have a problem. In fact, I have a barrowload of problems.'

Jerry fished a new notepad from his desk, flipped it open, engaged his ballpoint and, with frills, invited Cyril to list his problems in order.

'Shoot, Mr Breathstone. Problem number one.'

'Can't we leave number one till later, Mr. Quid?'

'Any sequence you like, sir, but – for my notes – I will number the problems in my notebook in the order you trot them out.'

'Won't that confuse things when eventually I get to number one?' enquired the client.

'How the hell – eh, pardon – how should I know the answer to that before you start. Surely, that goes without saying?'

'How can it go without saying when I haven't said anything?'

'BECAUSE you have so far said nothing, Mr Breathstone, EVERYTHING you haven't said goes without bloody saying. Now, what are you here for, or are you just sheltering from the rain?'

'I have a lot of problems, Mr Quid. Please try to be understanding. It would help if you'd start your notes by putting on your pad 'Problem number 5'.'

Jerry was on the point of exploding.

'I'm not Eric Morley, you know – and this isn't Miss World – we don't do things in reverse order here.'

'Reverse order? – oh, that reminds me of number 4 – two youths made improper suggestions to me in the public toilets at the beach.'

'So we start with number 4, then.'

Jerry had more than a suspicion that any improper suggestion in the Gents would be sponsored by Mr B. The lawyer scored out Nos 1 and 5 and started to write. '4. C.B. – lewd and libidinous in beach loo'.

'Next?' he invited.

'Number 5, Mr Quid – Someone's been stealing underwear from my clothes-line.'

Jerry felt the contents of his stomach make a jump for his throat, swallowed hurriedly and struggled to keep calm. The appropriate entry made on his notepad, he invited number 3.

'Let's make it number 2, Mr Quid – when I got back from the Gospel Hall last night, there were two strapping girls in my bed. I ran into the kitchen and prayed for strength to cope with the temptation.'

'Were your prayers answered?'

'I'll never know, Mr Quid. By the time I had got undressed, they ran away.'

This man is truly an idiot, thought Jerry – or maybe it's me who's the idiot for listening. But the whole thing was obviously so real to old Breathstone, and with only two problems to go Jerry elected to dour it out.

'Number 3?'

'Oh yes, number 3 – my neighbours keep banging on our dividing wall for hours every night. It's going for my nerves, and sometimes I have to take a wee drink before I can get to sleep.'

'I see,' said Jerry, noting it all down. 'And what about problem number 1?'

'Well, it's the police, Mr Quid. They've charged me in connection with the other four problems, and I wonder if it will go easier for me if I own up?'

Jerry rose to his feet, 'I think you should go, Mr Breathstone, and if you really want my advice, I think you should come back when you're sober.'

'Could you lend me a few pounds meantime, sir?'

'Good afternoon, Mr Breathstone,' choked Jerry, helping the gent into his wet clothes and showing him out.

Now, you may ask, what about Marjory Squeeze's pregnancy? Well, after all the attentiveness initially shown by Ray round about the time Duncan's daughter got married (incidentally, she also is expecting her happy event a few months after Marjory) normal behaviour was resumed without over-much delay. Poor Marjory's condition was largely ignored until it became impractical to ignore it any longer. Normally fastidious about her appearance, in comparison with Ray anyway, Marjory became dowdier month by month, and her husband's handicap had every opportunity to dip to 'scratch' so often did he find the need to seek sanctuary on the links. Marjory's mother did enough fussing for all of them, knitting, sewing, to-ing and fro-ing, all to the extent that the expectant father could be excused for thinking that nothing about the event was any of his doing. Not that he could remember whether it was or not.

November was the allotted month for his wife's delivery and, try as he did, Ray couldn't for the life of him remember what had prompted his aberration during the February preceding. However, when baby Roxanne popped her head out at the Maternity Unit, Ray was advised immediately, and he went to the car park straightaway on replacing the phone, detouring only slightly to finish the pint he had just ordered at the clubhouse bar.

'At least you got round in time, Ray,' spouted some nag. 'We might have had to call you in from the far end of the course!'

Ray found mother and baby were doing fine when he dashed breathless into the hospital. He had decapitated the hastily bought flowers as he slammed the car door, so that what he presented to his wife looked as if it had come out fresh from a tumble-drier.

'I suppose it's the thought that counts,' he grinned sheepishly as he held the mess towards the new mother.

Marjory took the fractured blooms and called a nurse to put into water anything that was left with a stem on it.

'Perhaps I can find a saucer somewhere,' the nurse smiled as she took the offering away.

'I've decided to call the baby Roxanne,' Marjory announced, searching Ray's eyes for a response!

'Rock Salmon? What in the name of …'

'Roxanne darling – ROXANNE,' she spelled it out.

'What on earth for? I thought you'd want to call her Euphasia after your mother, or something just as stupid. Come to think of it, Roxanne is just as stupid.'

Marjory burst into tears, an affliction to which she was subject even without the aggravation of post-natal exhaustion.

A severe looking staff-nurse cast her shadow over the bed-cover.

'I think you should go now, Mr Squeeze. Can't you see your wife is tired? Everything will seem better tomorrow.'

Ray kissed a salty tear off his wife's cheek.

'Everything will be all right, dear. Just you wait.'

As he turned to leave, Marjory sobbed, 'You'd better come in a better mood tomorrow or Roxanne and I will be even more upset.'

Ray screwed up his face as he left, the name 'Roxanne' burning his ears. He felt sure that the others in the ward were having a good chuckle about that idiotic name and worse still, were probably blaming HIM for having chosen it.

In the days following, Ray was good nature itself at work. It was 'Roxanne' this and 'Roxanne' that until he must have been the only person left in the world not sick with the very sound of the bloody name.

At the christening on Christmas Sunday, the full name was droned out by the Reverend Petty – called from retirement to officiate – 'And I baptise thee Roxanne – Euphasia Squeeze......'

'With a friggin hyphen too,' confided Jerry to Duncan after the Service. 'Poor little mite. I can just visualise it in the newspaper – "a sister for Jonquil Raymond and Myrnaloy-Jane"!'

Duncan eyed Jerry with mock sternness.

'People in glasshouses, Jerome Lenza, people in glasshouses, remember?'

Jerry blushed, took his wife Anne by the arm, and sped off for Christmas dinner.

But, the outcome of the pregnancy explained, it's back to events preceding the arrival of the juniormost Squeeze.

REVD. STELLA CUMMING

When Reverend Petty was finally led tottering to a local nursing home for spent minds, his successor as incumbent at St Artois Parish proved to be a truly delightful offspring from the union of the Equal Opportunities Commission and the more liberal faction of the National Church. Reverend Stella Cumming MA BD saw to it that much of what was traditional at the manse had vanished before moving in. Leather chairs and velvet curtains gave way to Sanderson co-ordinates downstairs, and pretty dolly mixture patterns adorned upstairs windows with more than a hint of Mary Quant. The Reverend lady, in her mid-thirties and married with two children soon took to driving round her parish in a scarlet Maserati, courtesy of her he-man husband who looked every bulging inch a gangster or gun-runner, but who in fact was innocuously in 'Insurance', if such a description is possible. Because Mr Cumming had been the recipient of considerable inherited wealth, Stella didn't want for anything and certainly wasn't in the Ministry for the money (who in their senses would be!)

So for this reason as well as for a patent dedication for saving lost souls, she threw herself enthusiastically into her new charge. Backed up by good looks, an engaging smile and infectious laughter, Stella Artois, as she quickly became affectionately known, intoxicated more than the regular worshippers at her church. Of course, as so often happens in church circles, Stella appealed to a new breed of worshippers and at the same time offended some of the 'old guard' who considered that a minister should be of mature years, bald, dignified, sombre, pliable and, above all, male. Stella had none, but none, of these prerequisites, so there were a number of disjunctions and membership-transfers elsewhere among the older spinsterhood. But most of the older 'marrieds' remained loyal, not least because the husbands (whatever they may have muttered among themselves) really quite enjoyed their Sunday eyeful. Stella knew what she was letting herself in for from day one, and none of the shifts in congregation pattern came to her as any surprise; she well knew that her popularity in some circles had more to do with the flesh than the spirit. However, being well conversant with the parable of the talents, Stella used all that she had to pursue the Lord's business, and if this meant flaunting what the Lord had given her, then flaunt it she most certainly would – and did!

Many of her members, only intermittent attenders at Sunday services hitherto, became re-charged with ecclesiastical zeal, and Duncan, Ray and Jerry were in this group. They even took to discussing sermons and church affairs during their odd tea-break togetherness, but perhaps not in terms of which the clergywoman herself would have approved.

'Bloody good service that yesterday,' spat Ray, with cream from his meringue adhering to his ill-shaven chin.

'Nice sermon,' added Duncan, de-misting his glasses.

'Nice blouse,' mused Jerry 'Good to see a Minister who has dress-sense for a change.'

'I wonder why she doesn't wear a robe, or gown or whatever you call it?' queried Duncan.

'That's a damn stupid observation if you ask me,' muttered Ray, cleaning his chin with the back of his hand. 'If she wore a gown, she might as well shave her head and sing bass!'

'I can see church-going has hardly sanctified your thoughts, boys – there's more to church attendance than ogling the minister,' smiled Jerry.

'There *used* to be more to it,' replied Ray promptly, 'but it's bloody hard to look at that woman and think pure. I tried looking at the stained glass, the carved pillars, the organ pipes ... I even shut my eyes and tried to concentrate on what she was saying. But every time my eyes were drawn back to the pulpit, my concentration shifted from her sound to her sight.'

'Maybe we should campaign to have her removed because she is damaging the community's spiritual welfare then?' enquired Jerry.

'Not bloody likely,' sprayed Ray, having just sipped some lukewarm tea. 'I'll take my chances with any God that has *her* as His spokesperson!'

'Well, just watch what chances you take, Raymond. Her husband doesn't look like he bathes in the milk of human kindness!'

'By the way,' awakened Duncan, 'Old Petty wants me to make a new will for him. I'll be most of the afternoon at Bide-a-wee or whatever you call his rest home. Do you think he has enough of his marbles left to give any rational instructions?'

'If he says he wants to leave all his money to Stella,' winked Jerry, lighting a fag, 'then he's the sanest man on earth!!'

'Here! Here!' grinned Ray.

THE ROTARY LUNCH

Piddletown Rotary Club is made up of self-employed business folk from a whole variety of trades and professions who down-tools for lunch together once a week – in the case of Piddletown each Wednesday. That day the cocktail lounge of Queens Hotel witnesses the ritual of fifty year old (on average) men (no ladies as yet, folks) shambling through the plate-glass doors anytime from noon, and thence to the dining-room for one o'clock lunch away from the bar-lunch casuals.

The customary proceedings entail a pre-lunch blether over an aperitif, a rather ordinary three course meal preceded or followed by grace, a toast to the monarch of the day, coffee and lighting up of smoking materials, the president's ten minutes of business prompted by an able secretary at hand, perhaps some reporting from committee convenors, announcements of one kind or another – and then the introduction of the weekly 'guest speaker'. This Wednesday, the guest speaker is 'Duncan Smile Esq., Bachelor of Law, Notary Public, Senior Partner of that well known local law firm of Henry Chancer and Company. Mr Smile is a familiar face to all but the very newest of our members – indeed he has done legal work for many of you. The fact that Mr Smile's clients here are still in business says something for his competence as a solicitor. But that's enough introduction for a man who needs no introduction. So, without further ado, I am pleased to ask Mr Smile to address you on his chosen subject "Being a Senior Partner".'

Duncan blew his nose strongly, rose weakly as if exhausted, smiled inanely, cleared his throat, and began – hands sweating and atremor, clutching some dirty papers torn off a lined notepad.

'Mr President, fellow guests, Rotarians and friends – it's no easy matter being a senior partner in a Law Firm. Not one minute of the day is mine. Waking and sleeping, responsibility presses in like a vice against my temples and a weight on my shoulders …'

True enough, as if by magic large beads of perspiration squeezed out the pores of his face, and his shoulders hunched forward visibly. The sudden ageing process, for a fraud like Duncan, was pure RADA stuff, and one could almost reach out and touch the wave of sympathy which rolled across his rapt audience.

'... and all the time the pain, the gnawing pain in the vitals, the throbbing head and the irregular thumping of the heartbeat; the worry – worry about and on behalf of stricken clients, the nervous anxiety to do and say all the right things at the right time; the fear that my standards of professional excellence may not be matched by my junior partners – what if their inexperience or downright carelessness undoes all that my life has been spent in building up? And I'm not a well man, gentlemen ...'

At this point Duncan paused, unscrewed a small bottle, popped a couple of white pills on his furred tongue theatrically, and swished them down with the remnants of his red wine. Swaying slightly with eyes half-closed, Duncan had played one sympathy-card too many. The bevvy of Rotarians were getting restless, checking their watches and started muttering among themselves.

'... day in, day out, in all weathers, no matter how I feel, I must present myself at my place of business because I owe it to my staff and, indeed to the whole community. What would happen, I ask myself, if I failed to show up at my desk? Could I rely on anyone in my office to pick up the pieces and solve all the problems? As I said to the Young Mothers' Group ...'

The Town Hall clock struck 2 o'clock. There is an unwritten rule at Piddletown and other Rotary Clubs, that the Speaker can talk as long as he likes, but everyone else leaves at 2 p.m. sharp to open their own shops, offices or whatever. A shuffling of feet signified the departure of the first half-dozen, of whose absence Duncan was oblivious. By the time half the Rotarians had gone – on tiptoe, feigning invisibility, Duncan had twigged to some movement. The President, Secretary, and eight past service (retired) members alone remained to hear Duncan's winding up.

'And so, Gentlemen, do not envy me. How well I remember having envied my seniors when I was young. Now I envy them. Their comfort and peace in the local cemetery. If I had the chance to live my life again, I would not come back as a senior partner!'

Having so said, Duncan lifted his empty glass, and sucked a bit of sediment noisily as he sat down, rubbing his forehead with his cuff.

Hollow insincere clapping from ten sets of geriatric hands brought the President to his feet.

'Fellow Rotarians, unfortunately Rotarian Jackson – who was to have proposed the vote of thanks – had to leave on urgent business, as have some others. Those who could not wait to the end of Mr Smile's address missed a real treat, and I ask you to accord the club's thanks to our guest in the time-honoured manner.'

Arthritic hands again stirred into half-hearted action, and, with but a hurried handshake from the president, Duncan was left alone in the dining-room.

Duncan noticed one or two not-quite-empty wine glasses around him, slipped the contents of each furtively over his throat and hunched out into the rain, the Granada, and the office.

'How did it go?' enquired Jerry on his return.

'Very well, I think,' replied Duncan. 'Always keen to do a public relations job for the firm. Wouldn't be surprised if a fair amount of new business comes from it. You guys should take more of your share. You can't expect me to keep spellbinding all the local clubs – one of these days I might lose my touch.'

'I wonder what the bastard told them?' Ray later queried to Jerry over coffee.

'Nothing they're likely to remember – I hope!!'

Duncan went home exhausted at 3.30 p.m. and had himself a stiff brandy, then phoned the Rotary President to say thanks for the club's hospitality and that he'd be happy to speak to the club again at any time.

'We'll certainly remember to contact you when a vacant date arises,' lied the bald president, picking long blonde hairs off his collar.

THE OPEN

Needless to say, towards mid-July, Ray's concentration on such trifling things as business took its annual knock. Especially with this year's British Open Golf Championship not only in the offing but in Scotland too, and rightly so. And near enough to reach in a forty-five minute drive.

'I might be missing next Friday afternoon,' he announced the week previous. In fact, Ray turned up at the office for an hour on the Tuesday morning and wasn't seen again until the following Monday. Only those who have sampled the 'Open' atmosphere – feet on the hallowed turf and mingling with the crowds – can imagine the magnetism of the occasion. Of course, we can all see much more on television, and without all the traffic jams, parking ordeals, soakings and buffetings – and without the sheer exhaustion which hits after straining over hillocks, hummocks and dunes, through whins, gorse and barbed wire – all for a glimpse of favourite performers and to rub elbows with a celebrity. That exhaustion stays its hand during all the excitement of the day out, and then wallops the back of the knees and grips the waist and buttocks when the weary trek to the car park is faced near day's end. And there are those like Ray, first in their hundreds and then in their tens of thousands, who spend all the daylight that God gives tramping the course or weaving in and out of the hospitality areas, not only on the four days of the Championship proper, but on the preceding four days of practice to boot. Autograph hunters swarm the practice days and, dependent on the availability or the show of courtesy, or lack of it by the 'stars' approached, book in hand, the good guys and the bad guys among the golfers gain affection or disfavour in a twinkling.

On the Wednesday, Ray got himself near enough to Ballesteros and Nicklaus that even Ray himself was surrounded by a group of wee boys with autograph books and signed the first book with a smile.

'You're not wan of them!' yelled the first boy, squinting at Ray's scrawl, tearing out and crumpling the page in disgust.

True enough, he was approached by a middle-aged American lady as she emerged from the Champagne and Oyster Tent, but by the time Ray had got his pen out she had fainted in a crumpled heap. After hurriedly checking his flies, it clicked with Ray that the lady had been overcome by the champagne, the oysters, the heat or by all three, and elected to vanish on the basis that he'd rather be charged with lack of chivalry than with assault. Had he known that the lady was an internationally renowned film star, he might have risked giving her the kiss of life, in the hope of getting a mention buy the media – or even a reward. At least, to have offered this service would have topped up his alcohol level. He missed the chance, but to this day claims to know her well.

Ray felt very much at home among the golfing and showbiz fraternity. He giggled when any of the big names said anything at all – and most of what they said was inane at best and downright boring otherwise. But there's always a coterie of hangers-on who hang on every word of the 'mighty' as if each was endowed with a special wisdom akin to Holy Writ – and Ray was such a person on such an occasion.

'Did you hear what Trevino just said?' chortled Ray to a stranger at his elbow, struggling to avoid a dose of mirthful pant wetting.

'Yes, isn't he the greatest!' came the reply from his neighbour, whose puzzled smile confirmed that he also hadn't heard a thing of interest.

The massive galleries on the main days heaved with enthusiasts, experts, semi-experts, pseudo-experts, self-styled experts and hosts of non-experts simply there to enjoy the occasion, and the usual barrage of posers who, at the 'Open', more than anywhere else except at a Royal Garden Party, are there to be seen. In the tented village, and being trailed around on sponsored buggies, dozens of dolly-girls flashed their teeth, their bosoms, their thighs and anything else of commercial merit and all looked thoroughly decorative for the moment of the passing glance. A longer look at some would disclose the emptiness in the eyes of these beautiful bodies, hired for their looks and availability, many showing the wear and tear of masculine and alcoholic abuse which thick make-up did nothing to disguise. The shops stocked with the most expensive clothing and equipment sold out like there was no tomorrow, mostly to Americans, who seemed to be in competition as to who spent most money.

A real occasion right enough, but a real occasion full of artificial jollity, artificial know-how and artificial people – all of whom at close of day had to battle home to the real world of the semi, the flat, or the dole, heady with the scent of wealth but owning nothing but their memories of the affluence of others. A winner earning tens of thousands for playing a week's golf held in love and awe by people who'd normally abhor the cheek of a neighbour who'd have the gall to earn £20,000 in a whole year. All the throng, sharing in the winner's millions without touching a penny of it – indeed paying for the privilege of doing so – indulging without any real envy (so unreal is everything associated with being paid a fortune to enjoy oneself) in applauding the success of others – and no bad thing too.

Ray's 'Open' was a huge success. He pushed his children into the paths of celebrities to coax their signatures on to the glossy over-priced programmes. He nearly managed to lose Marjory in the crowds so to sidle into juxtaposition with lissom girls with tight bottoms and thrusting tops. But always Marjory found him, or the children tugged at the tail of his anorak to demand attention. They knew him well enough not to demand money, which in any event he'd have forgotten to bring with him, but the flavour, the glamour and the racing pulse overcame all distractions, and seeing crisp one-irons drilled 300 yards to the base of a distant flagstick has a lingering delight which other pleasures of the flesh cannot match – or so Ray tells us, probably in truth to him.

And in these hallowed circumstances, finely honed palates can eat the uttermost muck and imbibe the foulest booze and still elate as if nurtured by food and drink of the Gods. Such is the hypnotic spell that covers the vast acreage and all its population in a roseate hue of euphoria. Except, perhaps, in the toilets which, in spite of the most fastidious of attention, are still just toilets, in which any who actually enjoy themselves deserve a wide berth from other users. But it takes all sorts, and all sorts are to be found at such an event. As witness the gent who got no sympathy from the police officer to whom he reported the artful 'fumbling' of his diamond-encrusted watch.

'Serves you right, sir, for bringing here anything so valuable,' rebuked the constable. 'You left civilisation behind you when you passed through the turnstiles, you know.'

More than having lost his watch, the gent was downright affronted on hearing mention of having entered the course by the public pay-boxes. Good God man, he had flown in by helicopter! What happened thereafter is not recorded. Almost certainly the watch was a goner, an Insurance Company was ripped off, and premiums would rise to foot the bill. And the gent would be but one of many who left the course lighter than when he arrived.

If the 'Open' is a mountain-peak of excitement, the Sunday evening when the crowds have gone is the flattest plain in the world. No sooner is the prizegiving concluded than the first of the big names zoom away. The lesser names have already gone. Mainland participants of the upper echelons depart in their Porches and Masaratis, overseas competitors via helicopter to the nearest international airport, and the chosen few by private jet on standby at a local runway.

Hotel foyers are jammed with porters, pockets stuffed with tips, whilst removing cases and clubs to waiting taxis and small aircraft which buzz away at a few hundred feet casting their final shadows over the week's deserted battleground to which fleets of lorries are trudging to commence the dismantling and removal of the grandstands.

By 9 p.m. all is quiet but for a few stragglers who wait over before hitting the morning Concorde to far-off lands, and another arena in which to battle, for the next week's bonanza bathed in the adulation of the next week's audience.

And so it goes, world-wide, year in, year out – and many of the posers go too, the professional hangers-on whose idea of a holiday would be a fortnight in the one place just about anywhere where golf isn't played. And such a place isn't easy to find.

Duncan and Jerry had their 'Open' too. Recorded highlights on the telly on Thursday and Friday and four-hour sessions on Saturday and Sunday afternoon. No crowds, no hassle, good clean food and drink. Well, at Jerry's, anyway!

On Monday, the rains cascaded down. Ray was in a foul mood,

blaming everyone for his own neglects of the week previous, arrogantly pacing round the office as if he had won the 'Open' whilst his colleagues and staff had squandered his winnings.

'Can't turn my back here for two minutes without you bastards letting me down!'

Not a word about the disasters averted by some uncharacteristic zeal employed by Jerry – and even by Duncan – whilst their partner played the big-shot. Not that Jerry and Duncan expected anything different. It is, after all, an annual event.

THE LATIN QUARTER

Ray lent back in his worn chair, feet on desk, arguing the toss with Jerry about a case in which, simultaneously, the former had been consulted by the husband, the latter by the wife.

'*Matrimonia debent est libera*' quoth Jerry.

'You don't say,' muttered Ray, unimpressed with Jerry's Latin maxim offered in support of his lady client's philanderings. Realising that Ray hadn't a clue what it meant – any more than had Jerry before he 'looked it up', Mr Quid explained

'Marriages ought to be free, my son!'

'Don't you 'my son' me, Aristotle. Even though by nature I always assume a *media sententia* (i) posture, that doesn't give your client the right to piss about after her marriage. All your bloody Latin maxim means is that a coerced marriage is a bad one.'

Which just about got it right, surprisingly.

'Exactly, Mr Squeeze. Your self-righteous prig of a husband coerced my client into marriage by putting her up the spout – so it WAS a bad marriage on your own admission. *Medio tempore* (ii), my client *est libera* (iii) and doesn't intend to be subject to your client's enforced *NEXUS* (iv)'

'Oh shut your Roman face, big nose – my client is suing his wife for divorce on the grounds of her misconduct, and there's no good you trying to flex bogus intellectual muscle in front of me – send the woman packing. There's no way we can act for them both. Their interests are in total conflict. Now show me some *sana mentis* (v) and give us both peace.'

'I shall do *secundum bonum et aeguum* (vi) as usual,' snapped Jerry, and closed the door on leaving, so to give his partner peace to practise putting on his new carpet.

'He's getting worse,' mused Ray to himself, and then, absentmindedly he backswung his putter through the glazed door of the nearby bookcase, so that as the ball propelled forward the fragmented pane exploded *simul et semel* (vii)

'*Res fit bloodyinjuria*,' (viii) he cursed to himself.

i. Middle view
ii. Meantime
iii. Is free
iv. Imprisonment
v. Common-sense
vi. According to what's fair
vii. At the same time
viii. That's what bloody happens when you take your eye off the ball.

INDECENT EXPOSURE

Miss Nibbs had sat for a good forty minutes in the waiting room. Like someone straight from an early silent film, Miss Nibbs was the complete model spinster, dressed in black from her veiled hat to her buttoned shoes, the solid blackness of her broken only by her thin white face and whiter lips, ill-fitting pre-war dentures and a tuft of white hair on her chin.

Embarrassed by her continuing presence as other clients came and went, Jerry strolled along to Duncan's room to remind him, in case he had forgotten that the lady was there. Duncan was white-inking out a score of errors in his secretary's single-page effort and waved Jerry out of his room with an irritated assurance that he knew all about Miss Nibbs and would see her when he was good and ready.

'And, by the way, Duncan,' said Jerry as he left, 'your flies are undone!'

'Bloody cheek,' muttered Duncan continuing his repair-work, ignoring Jerry's warning as just another of his junior's idiotic jests. Five minutes later, Duncan yawned and rose, admired his artwork, then strolled nonchalantly towards the waiting room, trousers handsomely agape.

'Come away in, Miss Nibbs,' boomed the senior. 'Sorry to have kept you waiting – a rushed job, you know. Priorities first, m'dear!'

He waved Miss Nibbs past and ahead of him. In spite or because of her eighty-five years of unadulterated spinsterhood, nothing could restrain Miss Nibbs furtive glance towards the lawyer's lower abdomen, a glance which Duncan didn't notice. Indeed, instead of sitting behind his desk as was his custom, Duncan on this occasion ambled over towards the window area of his room, turned and sat himself on the 'nightstore' heater for inner warmth, his legs apart with his shirt-tail spilling over on to his left thigh. Miss Nibbs hardly knew where to look, but did so just the same.

'Now what can I do for you, my dear?' the lawyer enquired.

'Well, I'm nervous to go to the police, Mr Smile, and wondered if you would do so for me?'

'I see,' replied Duncan, rising and at the same time thrusting his hands into his trouser pockets, thus forcing his zip down its final inch. 'And what do you want me to tell the police, Miss Nibbs?'

'I want you to tell the police that I am being bothered by a man.'

Good God, thought Duncan – the old bitch is suffering from delusions.

'Bothered, Miss Nibbs. In what way?'

'Well, there's an elderly gentleman in the flat across from mine, and he's taken to ringing my doorbell at nights.'

Well what are you complaining about, thought Duncan to himself.

'There's no crime in ringing your bell, Miss Nibbs. Maybe he's a caring soul who wants to check that all's well with you before he turns in for the night?'

'I think not, Mr Smile, because when I open the door, the man is standing like …'

'Like what, Miss Nibbs?'

'Like THAT!' replied the spinster, pointing at Duncan's trousers.

Duncan's eyes followed the lady's boney forefinger to his crotch, saw his own indecent exposure, yanked violently at his zip which jammed in his shirt-tail.

'Good God Almighty!' exploded Duncan. 'Why didn't any sod tell me about this! – Oh sorry, Miss Nibbs, I didn't mean to frighten you. This has been a horrible mistake. Please accept my unreserved apology. I feel utterly ashamed.'

'That's funny, Mr Smile. Those are exactly the words my neighbour uses – every time he docs it!'

'How disgusting for you,' drooled Duncan, his face bursting with embarrassment. 'Of course I'll speak to the police for you, certainly I will.'

'Thank you Mr Smile – will you be asking the Police to take your own offence into account?' she smiled, knowingly.

Duncan blushed again, apologised again, and yet again, fawning all the way and promising swift action.

'Had YOU been my neighbour, Mr Smile, I may not have complained!'

Duncan winced, saw Miss Nibbs out to the pavement, and then made a knock-kneed beeline for the gents to repair his discomfiture.

'Told you,' winked Jerry as they nearly collided in the passage. 'Bastard!' whistled Duncan in response.

THE HYDRO

For ten years they had been talking about it. Usually when intemperate. Daft notions frequently seem like good ideas when the edge of sobriety is dulled. A good reason, presumably, for a clear head when making decisions. The new Building Society Office 'Champagne Welcome' had sweetly confused Duncan, Jerry and Ray as they found themselves together on the pavement sunshine after their valedictory 'Thank you' comments to the new Branch Manager.

'Well,' swayed Duncan 'How about that weekend away with our wives that we've always promised ourselves?'

'Great idea,' slurred Ray, with an enthusiasm wholly out of character.

Jerry just nodded, having heard it all before, but doubting whether either of his partners relished having their respective Doreen and Marjory in tow for any longer than it took to drop them off somewhere. Indeed, Jerry positively gasped when Ray continued.

'No time like the present, boys. I'll phone the Hydro right now and book three double rooms. Lend me some coins for the phone.'

Ray never carried money in case he had to part with it. Armed with fives and tens, Ray took off to the call box in the Square and left his colleagues both surprised and amused in the evening sun. A few minutes later, Ray emerged, still smiling, and halfway to rejoining the others, beamed broadly.

'So you clowns thought I was incapable of making decisions. We're booked from Friday week till Sunday after lunch. I gave your name, Duncan; it's easier to spell! You've to write confirming with a £60 deposit. Tell them we'll arrive at 6.30 p.m. – you know, for drinkies before dinner.'

'Good for you, Raymond,' smiled Jerry. 'I must …'

'Oh,' interrupted Ray, 'There's an open golf competition, including Hydro guests – thirty six holes on the Saturday, and the three of us are booked to take part. After all, we don't want to spoil the ladies' weekend, do we, by forcing our presence on them all the time?'

'Crafty devil,' chuckled Duncan, not himself a keen golfer, but sharing Ray's thoughtfulness about avoiding any over-imposition on the womenfolk.

After a round of quite unnecessary handshakes, the three split up and two of them taxied to their respective homes, still with a measure of sparkle in each bloodstream.

Jerry was first home. Anne was hosing the front garden as Jerry opened the gate.

'Howdy, lover,' he greeted Anne as he crossed the lawn.

Anne propped the hose into a fork in the large cherry tree so that the jet was angled down the length of rockery in glorious weed-free bloom.

'Hello you,' she replied cheerfully. 'Had a good evening?'

'Most interesting,' smiled Jerry, removing his tie as if to swap the formality of the day for a taste of the holiday atmosphere which fine weather does much to induce. 'You'll never guess what. We are having a sixsome at the Hydro at the end of next week!'

'With the Squeezes and Smiles? You must be joking. That's great – well it's great to get a weekend away! How did this come about?'

'Free drink, that's how, pet!'

'Well I never! Let me put the hose off and we'll go round the back and catch the rest of the sun on the terrace and chat about it. Like a cool drink with ice?'

'Now you're talking, Annie. You get the drinks and I'll shove on a short sleeved shirt.'

An hour later, the sun sank slowly and the air chilled. Anne and Jerry went indoors, enjoyed a late grill and eventually climbed the stairs and fell asleep smiling.

Duncan banged the front door shut. His eyes still unfocussed in the dark hallway after leaving piercing sunlight, he tripped over Doreen's anorak which lay on the worn hall carpet and called out, 'Doreen, it's me. Where are you?'

Doreen skipped downstairs and planted a kiss on her husband's stubbled cheek.

'Not just now, Doreen. I've something to tell you before dinner.'

'What dinner, Duncan? I thought you were eating out?'

'Eating out nothing – unless you mean these savouries and petit fours that we got. Thought we'd have a steak and a bottle of red wine.'

'I've nothing ready,' writhed Doreen. 'Maybe something from the Chinese would do. I'll go if you want.'

'Sit down woman. You can go after I've stopped talking.'

Doreen sat down.

'That's better. Now, I'm taking you away for a wee holiday to the Hydro, the weekend after this. I know you'll like this. The only snag is that I told Ray and Jerry of my intentions, and, dammit, they are talking of doing the same thing – copy cats! They probably felt ashamed that I was the only one planning a treat for his wife. However, I suppose we should be glad that my kindly gesture to you has rubbed off on the others.'

'It's typical of you to be so thoughtful, Duncan. I'm sure Marjory and Anne will be grateful.'

'Not a word to them, mind. Marjory and Anne should be left to think that it is THEIR husbands who have been the thoughtful ones.'

'You're a saint, Duncan. Always thinking of the happiness of others.'

'Good. That's settled. Now you get off to the Chinese and I'll get into my smoking jacket and check the wine cellar for something suitable. Your anorak is on the hall floor.'

'Thank you, dear, I won't be long.'

'Take your time, Doreen, there's boxing on the telly.'

Ray was the only one to drive home from the Building Society Office. He skilfully missed the kerb, the gatepost and the gate as he weaved into the driveway. Only a violent emergency stop one-inch from the garage door – spraying gravel like the wash from the QE II – betrayed hazy attention.

On his way to the front door, Ray stopped off to give an affectionate hug to his two children, who had been cutting the heads off flowers with his wedding cutlery. Marjory was in her sewing room, darning holes in an ancient golfing jumper. Ray had instructed his wife to do her best with his old clothes on the basis that 'they don't make them like that any more'.

Marjory didn't raise her eyes as Ray entered the room; he was still wearing his knee-length sheepskin coat in spite of the soaring temperature.

'Do you want a drink, or have you had one?' enquired the lady, still darning.

'Both, ' replied Ray, fumbling in the lining of his coat for his crumpled cheque book. He lent on the sewing machine and scribbled out 'Pay Mrs Marjory Squeeze ten pounds only' and signed then tore off the cheque and floated it on to his spouse's lap.

'Get a new outfit, dear – we're going on holiday Friday week.'

'What kind of outfit am I going to get for ten pounds? And where are we going on holiday?'

'Maybe I can make it a bit more, dear. And the answer is to the Hydro. I thought you needed a break and fixed things up today so you'd have something to look forward to.'

'That's nice of you, Ray, but what about the children?'

'Well, it's either your mother or boarding kennels, take your pick.'

'I'll try mother first if you don't mind. Get that drink you're talking about – you'll need it – it's you who's going to ask mother this time.'

'God, woman, there's not enough drink in a pub to get me phoning that creature. I've booked the holiday, so you book the other. Now I'm going to get that drink – come and tell me what's what when you've phoned.'

'Oh very well, but take that stupid sheepskin off or you'll melt. I'll pour you a bath before you have your pickled herrings.'

'Pickled herrings!' Ray grimaced, clutching his stomach.

The Hydro was like so many of its kind. An immense four-storey façade with an elegant sweep of broad stone steps outside from the parking area to tiers of gardens on various descending levels to lawns, and thence to the site of the disused railway which formerly boasted a private station for Hydro patrons their staffs and cabin trunks only. Being a relic of a bygone era, car parking facilities were not a feature of the place, and the winding tree lined driveway was nowadays parked solid along one side with everything from the odd new Rolls to the rusted ten year-olds. The driveway widened at the pillared entrance to the establishment itself, for the parking in which location there was always something of a rush, car-people as a breed being lazy about walking any further than is avoidable.

The trio of provincial lawyers, by pure chance and without having seen each other en route from Piddletown, coasted up the driveway in convoy –

Duncan's Granada, Ray's Rover and Jerry's over-the-hill Daimler – just in time to see a coachload of Americans (and the three parking lots which it had occupied) drawing out from just adjacent to the Hydro entry. The three cars turned in unison as if joined, and waltzed into the three adjoining spaces like formation dancers.

Ray was first out, flung open his car-boot, and caressingly rescued his precious golf clubs from amid a conglomerate of vintage Antler cases and polythene bags. In fairness, he did take a small case as well as the golf bag, and headed up the carpeted and flower-decked staircase, leaving two of the heavier, though less important, items for his wife's attention. Marjory and the four others plodded up some minutes behind, the whole party congregating in front of the long reception desk presided over by a couple of dolly-birds in crisp white blouses – and a couple of uniformed porters looking like corporals in a county regiment circa World War I.

Ray had abandoned his luggage in order to check if the lounge bar had moved since his previous visit some fifteen years earlier. Having found that all was well, he joined the others as Duncan was announcing their arrival to one of the blouses.

'Mr Smile. Ah yes, that's right, party of six. We have you in adjoining rooms on the first floor – 123, 125 and 127 – here are your keys. The porters will help you with your bags once you have registered. Each of the men registered, and Ray and Duncan followed their porter. Duncan saw to the tipping because Ray found that he had no change.

Jerry and Anne carried a small case each, having left all else in the car.

There were chuckles of delight all round as each room was entered and heartily approved, all to the front, still warm from the day's sunshine and southerly exposure and all enjoying a superb view over the terraced gardens to the pine trees and hills beyond.

Time 6.45 p.m., and agreement reached to rendezvous in the cocktail lounge at 7.45. Ray was back in the corridor at 6.50, having used his passkey to operate the automatic drinks machine, naively thinking the system to be complimentary and seeking out the ice dispenser whilst Marjory was unpacking. Jerry and Anne were subtler, one of their two cases being nothing short of a mobile bar for the duration of their stay.

Jerry's visit to the corridor in his dressing gown at 7.10 was for ice only, he and Anne having already showered. Duncan, as befitting the senior member, had phoned room-service and was the recipient of a flunkey-toted ice-bucket which chilled a bottle of something labelled champagne, but which would be more accurately described as fizzy wine judging by its modest price. Duncan had, however placed his order with some flourish, and the waiter nodded appreciatively at the £1 tip.

This being a day of coincidences, the doors of 123, 125 and 127 opened simultaneously at 7.40 as if operated from a single electronic switch, and out stepped three elegantly gowned ladies followed by three lounge-suited gents.

'That's good timing,' observed Ray. 'Can't wait for a drink.'

'Don't talk nonsense, Ray,' snapped his wife. 'You've just had three. You can't possibly be thirsty – and for goodness sake do up your tie.'

'I was thinking of a drink for YOU, dear,' Ray replied unenthusiastically.

'How kind, dear,' she snarled, and the two of them swept down the staircase ahead of the others.

Duncan and Jerry winked to each other, and walked in step together behind their spouses, not venturing any comment. By the time they entered the cocktail lounge, Ray and Marjory were smiling again, having secured a large corner table enough for the six of them and a large button-backed couch in velour with matching easy chairs.

'I'd have ordered drinks,' Ray lied 'but didn't know what would appeal to you girls.'

Ignoring Ray's feeble attempt at affability, Duncan saw that all except himself were seated, waved to an available cocktail waitress who was cleaning behind her nails with a swizzle-stick, and then himself sat down. The waitress approached without any easement of her bored expression, and Duncan invited her to take the orders of his party and put it on the bill for Room 123. Ray's face momentarily went ashen till he realised that he and Marjory were in 127.

'Good lad, Duncan,' piped Ray. 'Mine's a very large gin and tonic with ice and lemon.'

The Hydro

The waitress had started to write when Duncan interjected.

'Score that out, dear. Ladies first.'

Anne, Marjory and Doreen named their chosen tipple, and the waitress looked towards Duncan on each occasion as if to seek permission to write it down. Then Jerry, then Duncan himself. Ray sat quietly looking like a puppy waiting for permission to bark.

'And a very large gin and tonic with ice and lemon for my fat friend in the corner,' Duncan concluded.

All smiled, including Ray at last, and settled down to the customary activity of criticising the mannerisms, or the dress, or the hair of other patrons in the lounge. In what seemed to be a lifetime later, the surly waitress returned with a full tray, and dispensed the drinks. Another round, billed to Room 125, and the chat had become very relaxed indeed, if a shade disorganised. Time 8.20 – Ray suggested that dinner would be a good idea, there being no time for another round, and had Marjory on her feet as he spoke.

'That's OK, mate,' said Jerry. 'You can buy the wine.'

'Good idea,' said Anne enthusiastically. 'After all, us girls have had hardly anything – and wee ones at that. A couple of bottles of good wine won't be lost on OUR palates, will it ladies?' The other two nodded appreciatively. Ray gulped …

The dining room was immense, with an arched ceiling and ornamental pillars with stucco figures and symbols. Table 12 was excellently placed, out of the mad rush of waiters to-ing and fro-ing in the kitchen area, and not too near the string trio whose instruments would have been none the worse of tuning.

Presumably on the basis 'in for a penny' Ray clenched his teeth and summoned the wine waiter. He scanned the four-page choice available for consideration. True, he gulped again audibly as he scanned the prices, but thought to himself that, if he was astute, he could level out any financial disparity over the weekend. And, in money matters, Ray was as astute as they come.

'Two bottles of 46 please.' Ray shut the winelist before anyone could get a hint of his choice or its price. 'And bill Room 127, please.'

The waiter wrote something on a pad and presented it to Ray for signing. Ray obliged.

'Now then,' said Duncan. 'What are you girls doing tomorrow when the three of us are golfing?'

'The three of you are WHAT?' shot Marjory and Anne in chorus.

'You mean,' continued Duncan, 'that neither of you has had the guts to tell your wives why we are here? YOU must have known, Marjory, what with Ray's clubs in your room.'

'It never dawned on me,' replied Marjory. 'Ray takes his clubs everywhere – even when he visits my mother.'

'Specially when I visit your mother, dear. If I take a few swings in her garden it's less likely I'll take a swing at her!'

'Now then, that'll do of that,' intervened Duncan. 'What about you, Anne – didn't Jerry say anything about golf?'

'Oh he may have – and maybe it's a good idea. After all, he gets too little fresh air for his own good.'

'That's settled then,' Duncan adjudicated. 'Us boys will golf, and we'll each give our wives a wad of banknotes to spend in town while we're away. How's about that?'

'We're all for that,' chorused the girls.

Ray blanched, and reached out his hand for his glass. It was empty.

'Where's that bloody wine, then?' he snapped.

The dinner was delightful, the wine was just drinkable and Ray, who asked that liqueurs should be billed to Duncan's Room 123, found that he was the only one to order one.

'That was a cheap round,' smiled Duncan. 'Next one's on Jerry, then it's your turn again, Ray!'

Ray's 'Suits me' was less than convincing.

'I think a nice walk under the stars would be nice, Jerry,' said Anne 'It'll clear your lungs of all that smoke.'

Jerry lit another fag as he ambled along the corridor towards reception, and joined Anne who was waiting for him on the terrace. An hour later, the lights were out in 123, 125 and 127. Five of the six persons were asleep. Ray was in the Snooker Room on to his second frame against an off-duty barman, with his large cigar perched next to a tumbler of de-luxe whisky on a window ledge.

Duncan awoke to a cloudless sky already warming to the second week of ceaseless sunshine. Birdsong pierced the silence as daylight broke. Jerry and Anne lay in silence listening to the awakening day, windows wide open to welcome the pure morning air.

'Sorry about the golf, honey.'

'Idiot,' replied Anne softly. 'I'm delighted you're taking the chance – and thanks for the money.'

'Enjoy your shopping, then.'

'I will,' yawned Anne.

Then both rolled off their backs and fell asleep again in total comfort until half past seven.

Duncan rose at 6 a.m., dressed and walked downtown for the good of his health and the morning papers. Doreen got up at 6.30, unpacked an iron from her case and freshened up the creases in Duncan's golf shirt and slacks. She then dressed, and met Duncan halfway back up the drive. They sat together on a bench at the topmost level of the gardens and each read a paper until Duncan decreed at 8 a.m. that it was time for breakfast.

Marjory wakened at 8 a.m. and found herself alone in bed. Ray was snoring in an armchair near the window, cuddling his golf bag affectionately.

At 8.45 the Granada loaded, three lawyers, full of bacon, eggs, sausage and fried pancakes, were on their way to the local Golf and Country Club, leaving the ladies at the breakfast table to their third coffee. The 'Country Club' bit was a bit ostentatious, accepting that, aside from the golf course itself, there was nothing but a putting green and a table-tennis table with one bat and no balls in the unpretentious wooden changing room. The notice board did show the pairings for the open competition, for which starting times had been posted in the Hydro itself.

Duncan was playing with a 2 handicap Anglican clergyman and a left-handed local dentist. Ray and Jerry were drawn together, their third being a professional racegoer enjoying some recreation between meetings. Duncan's threesome was a sedate affair. Each vied with the other as to who could play worst and the decision was made long before the eighteenth to scratch and skip the afternoon's possible embarrassment.

By contrast, Ray and Jerry were in the thick of battle after only five holes. Jerry played miles above himself and two under fours. Ray holed in one at the short fourth and was four under. Gairdner, the gambler, was two over, but claimed a handicap of 24. On the sixth tee, Gairdner took an immense wallet from the leg of his plus-fours and gave the others a quick sight at what looked like hundreds of ten pound notes, and then invited – '£1,000 says there'll be no more holes in one from any of us. And £1,000 says I'll have the best net score after 36 holes. Such is my confidence; you two need only stake £50 apiece if you disagree on either count. In other words, I'm offering you twenty to one on each of the bets.'

'Make it fifty to one on the 'hole in one' and you're on. That's still generous odds so far as you are concerned,' replied Jerry. 'The twenty to one on your winning among the three of us is OK.'

'Done!' smiled Gairdner.

'Done,' shivered Jerry.

They now HAD to do all thirty-six holes. Thank God Duncan didn't know about the betting, thought them both – he'd have had the word passed round like wildfire. They hadn't, however, reckoned on Gairdner's big mouth over lunch. After the morning round, the three scores were:

Squeeze	76 less 4 handicap	72
Quid	83 less 12 handicap	71
Gairdner	91 less 24 handicap	67

As Gairdner drove his playing companions to the Park Hotel for lunch in his silver Bentley, all three of them were oblivious to the Open Competition for which they had entered – their own potentially financial threesome crammed their minds to the exclusion of all else. The Bentley parked, a smiling Gairdner cut a swathe to the Hotel entrance followed by the trembling figures of Ray and Jerry who, in spite of their weight and height respectively, looked like dwarfs in comparison.

Gairdner ordered two bottles of best champagne and a trolley at reception for delivery to his suite and entered the lift beckoning the others to join him. In a few minutes, after being engulfed in armchairs in the gambler's sumptuous suite overlooking the river and its surrounding splashes of rhododendrons and azaleas, two waiters knocked and entered with ice buckets and a trolley smothered in smoked salmon, a variety of cold meats, masses of trimmings and a lower deck awash with soufflés and fruits.

'Just a snack, lads. Can't overload the system before the afternoon's hostilities. We haven't much time, so eat, drink and relax.'

Relax? Very probably!!

The conversation was artificial. Ray and Jerry knew nothing about racing and Gairdner was interested in nothing else, except winning, of course.

'Do you always win?' asked Jerry nervously.

'Usually,' came the unemotional reply.

'Do you accept cheques?' Ray weakened.

'Usually.'

'Do you ever NOT get paid?' Ray gulped.

'NEVER!' enthused Gairdner, lighting a cigar as he threw a box of Havanas in Ray's direction.

Both Ray and Jerry decided that, if to lose looked likely, they might as well lose in comfort, and it was only when the second bottle was finished that they noticed that Gairdner was still on his first glass. Feeling great, but with no justification, the 'boys' thanked their host for lunch and followed him back to the Bentley.

Whilst Ray and Jerry were making merry with Gairdner's hospitality, the gent himself had asked to be excused whilst he made a few phone calls from the adjacent room. To his Turf Accountant, it was surmised. But not so, as became clear shortly after the trio came in sight of the first tee, at which a fairish gallery had foregathered.

'Must be a celebrity somewhere,' observed Jerry, looking around the crowd for some maybe familiar face. 'Maybe some Yank pro, or someone from films passing through and snatching a few holes.'

As Ray and Gairdner left Jerry tying his shoelace, the gallery opened and made a path for them, and burst into animated applause. There must have been a couple of hundred men, women and children, wearing bright summery colours and cheery faces as if handpicked by a camera crew for a telecast.

Gairdner was smiling affably, but not Ray who enquired angrily.

'What the hell's all this about, Mr Gairdner?'

'Oh nothing,' replied the gent, 'just told the press and a few friends that there's £5,000 riding on a hole in one and that a couple of sporting lawyers were trying to outgun Sir Barnabus Gairdner's 24 handicap for high stakes. Quite a lot of people know me, lads, it's obvious you've never heard of me!'

'You've got a bloody nerve, Gairdner, conning us into this set-up,' shot Jerry.

'No one's conned you, sonny,' replied Gairdner caustically. 'Neither my reputation nor knighthood was known to you when you agreed the stakes. The bet was among three golfers on the basis of five holes played and the assessment that each of us made of the others. Incidentally' – and at this point Gairdner raised his voice so that all could hear, 'the hole in one at 50 – 1, £100 staked, applies to all of us – I get £5,000 from between these two gentlemen if an ace falls to lucky me – isn't that real sporting of them both?'

Applause echoed through the trees, giving neither Ray nor Jerry a chance to challenge this extension to the engagement. In any event, the gallery had come to look like spectators at a cock-fight baying for blood. And lawyers in line to be ripped off attract little sympathy, being in something akin to a role-reversal situation. The two of them could smell hostility all around.

Jerry's pack of fags was empty at the tenth tee, by which time he had covered the front nine in 42, Gairdner in 50 and Ray in 36. Things were levelling out. Funny, the 'hole in one' was the big scare, and yet almost impossible to achieve. Well, Ray wasn't likely to get two in the one day and the other two players were simply not good enough to have any reasonable expectation.

Right to the penultimate green, the winner with the best net score was wide open, and this was one of these older country courses with a par 3 finish. Tension was not only gripping Ray and Jerry, but now also the whole crowd, which had doubled in size on the way round and surrounded not only tee and green, but also lined both sides of the tree-lined fairway. The tight avenue of trees and sea of faces both welcomed and scared at the same time.

A big oak overhung the left of the green, where the flag nestled behind a cavernous bunker. Only Gairdner looked calm, and he was first to play. Beads of sweat ran off at least two brows, and rivers of warm water ran down at least two backs.

Gairdner teed up and drew out a seven iron. Jerry looked skywards to where a lark hovered, making the only noise around.

'Whoosh' – Gairdner's ball shot skywards, bang on line. Gasps of 'Ooh' and 'Ah' rippled through the crowd as the ball seemed to hang above the flagstick.

'Good shot,' said Jerry involuntarily, then bit his tongue.

As the ball began its painfully slow decent, its glittering whiteness showed against the dark leaves of the oak, still on line. Only eight feet from the ground, the ball was arrested with a sharp crack as it collided with an overhanging branch, veered left, and splashed harmlessly into the bunker like a spent clay-pigeon.

Jerry and Ray held clammy hands like kindergarten kids and sighed with almighty relief. The crowd, kindled with sympathy, broke into open cheering which was as welcome to Squeeze and Quid as a pools win. It also relaxed them to the point of believing that anything was possible. Jerry next. Hooked slightly, hit same tree, landed on green ten feet from pin.

Ray fiddled with his grip and his feet, and took a couple of practice swings, smiled to the crowd, recomposed himself and took deliberate aim and set his nine iron out to the right of the green with a cultured draw.

Seconds later, the ball made soft contact with mossy greensward three yards passed the hole, popped forwards six inches then screwed back in a spiral straight for the hole. The crowd yelled encouragement as the ball clawed its way towards its goal – but it ran out of legs and stopped half-an-inch short.

As if at the final hole of the REAL 'Open', the gallery made a beeline for vantage points around the green, so what happened next was out of sight of the three golfers. Suffice to say that, with all the rush and excitement, a two-year-old escaped from its pushchair, coggled across the green, picked up Ray's ball and dropped it in the hole. The embarrassed parent ran and grabbed the child, and disappeared into the crowd.

A greenside gap opened up for Gairdner, Quid and Squeeze in that order, and in breaking out into a further burst of tumultuous applause, it was patently clear that the crowd was enjoying its play-acting just as much as Jerry and Ray did also.

Gairdner's eyebrows shot up as if on springs when he spotted that Ray's ball was missing. He shouted something to the others, but only when the crowd went silent could his voice be heard. Then it positively boomed as he pointed to the area of the flagstick.

'Where the hell is the ball that was there?'

'It dropped in,' yelled one wag – and soon dozens of voices echoed 'It dropped in!'

'No it bloody didn't, you bunch of cheating bastards,' Gairdner bellowed.

'Oh yes it bloody did!' replied the unruly chorus.

Gairdner cursed and swore and huffed off to the bunker with golf-bag still ashoulder, kicked his ball out of the sand into the crowd and made to force his way through and away.

'Better pay up, you cheat,' shouted a voice from the far side. Gairdner turned around and turned beetroot.

'Cheat, is it? We'll see about that. I don't believe any of you swine – but here's some bloody money if it'll shut you up. I've got to go.'

And, amidst renewed cheering, Sir threw a pile of tenners towards Ray and Jerry, and bulldozed his way towards the carpark and out of sight.

Ray and Jerry picked up the notes and counted them at £1,500.

'Drinks all round with thanks from us both,' shouted Jerry at the top of his voice, as Ray made a grab to tug at his shirt disapprovingly. 'I'll give £500 to the bar steward – he'll see you all right, get ices for the children – there's the van,' pointing to the vehicle with the open hatch and an eager ice-cream salesman.

Ray and Jerry blushed through the 'three cheers', accepted a lift from a gentleman of the Press and were back at the Hydro at six o'clock having forgotten to register their competition cards, but with £500 in crisp new tenners tucked in each of their sweaty right hands.

There was no sign of Duncan or the ladies after a search of bedrooms, bars, swimming pools and lounges. When finally passing the reception desk, they spied a footsore quartet ascending the staircase from the forecourt, all carrying parcels. It was Anne who spoke.

'You must think we are dreadful leaving you all this time. We do hope you haven't been too bored without us. We'll explain about the parcels after we have bought you a large drink. We've been a wee bit extravagant.'

Still in a state of shock, Ray insisted that the drinks were on him. An extravagance he'd probably regret later when his blood pressure had returned to normal.

The sixsome, parcels and all, repaired to the cocktail bar for half an hour, relaxing into welcoming plush chairs and thoroughly enjoying the rest and the iced drinks. The conversation was general and genial, and whilst touching on the pleasure of golfing in the sunshine, its financial implications remained unmentioned, by prior agreement. This was Ray's idea. He wanted time to consider whether Marjory should get any of the money.

Ray's secret – even if HE could have kept it – was blown later when the six re-entered the cocktail lounge for their pre-dinner snifter. Several thirsty well wishers indulged some backslapping and guffawing when Ray and Jerry appeared. Jerry was relieved that he had come clean with Anne whilst changing for dinner.

'What's all this, Raymond?' enquired Marjory haughtily.

Drawing his wife out of earshot of the others, Ray whispered.

'I just won a few quid in the competition, that's all. Keep your mouth shut and I'll give you your whack. For God's sake, not a word – Jerry probably hasn't told Anne.'

'But I've spent all the money you gave me this morning, Ray.'

'I ask you, dear, am I the one to deny you anything. Just trust me.'

Marjory's brows unfurled as they joined the others. Duncan had already bought the drinks waiting on the table. The hangers-on dissolved and the table talk steered itself away to other things, much to Ray's relief.

'I hear there was a big crowd at the golf course this afternoon,' said Duncan later.

'I didn't notice,' lied Ray. 'I was in too much of a hurry to get back to see Marjory.'

'Pardon?' enquired Duncan with raised eyebrows. 'Just how much have you had to drink?'

PROSPECTS OF PARTNERSHIP

What is the difference between all the hundreds of highly qualified assistant solicitors in the legal profession and the elite who are their employers, the self-employed with their names adorning die-stamped letterheaded paper, the capacity to sign cheques, make decisions, claim all the credit and shunt all the blame, who come and go as they please, and who complain about over-work when they seem to be doing very little? Well, the difference is one of progression – part of the ageing process. Most lazy middle-aged lawyers were at one time zealous youngsters with a fire in the belly to kindle insatiable ambition.

What happens to the Olympic sprinter after he breasts the winning tape? He runs on for a little, his speed ever decreasing, and his eyes searching for the adulation of the crowd. Oh, he COULD run again as well or even better if he put his mind to it after a short rest. But, for the moment with applause filling his ears and amid the back-slapping and congratulations, he is a spent force.

So the young lawyer when he is assumed into partnership, for which hitherto he has been no more than a striving underling. Assumption into partnership is his (or nowadays her) equivalent to breasting the tape. Before assumption, the assistant goes flat out with the single-mindedness of a well-tuned athlete. Any competition for such promotion only sharpens his resolve and fastens his pace. Once over the line, however, the rosy glow takes over, and his desk is no longer a workbench but rather a place on which to rest his weary limbs. His chair becomes more comfortable and he sleeps better – even at night. Oh, he maybe COULD do it all again if he put his mind to it. But why on earth should he? And thus the seeds of future attitudes are sown, the die is cast and the imprint of that die never gets clearer but can only fade as time goes by. Peculiarly, however, as the fire of zeal burns lower, the ego grows like rampant bacteria, and the public is more impressed by the vague sweet-talk of a thinly varnished partner than it ever is when the words come from a mere assistant, no matter how sharply honed that assistant may be on all aspects of the business on hand. The partner is, in effect, a retired assistant.

And how come some make the transition easily and whilst young, while others remain longer, or even forever, as plodders in their master's office? Well, a lot of it is pure luck – being in the right place at the right time. Pubs and clubs throughout the land are littered with musicians and singers infinitely more talented than some who top the bill on network television. But luck has passed them by, and they eke out a living getting bald and fat, frequently ending their professional careers propped up, or keeled over, by the sympathy or alcohol dispensed by customers who never knew how good they used to be. If the brilliant pianist isn't spotted when young and personable, he'll end up as accompanist to a tenth-rate chanteuse. So with the lawyer.

Farquhar had no intention of accompanying anyone. He had set his early sights on being a soloist, and he was certainly in the right place at the right time with Messrs Chancer. All three partners at Chancers' were middle aged, to put it kindly, and each was some thirty years out of University and by this much out of touch with things academic. Law Journals, Acts of Parliament and other Law Society news-sheets and books were piled up on filing cabinets un-opened except when Farquhar read them. Advice was passed on from junior to seniors more than vice versa and that Farquhar was becoming indispensable was lost on no one.

So Farquhar didn't need to ask what was in store for him. In mid-November, he was called into Duncan's room, where Ray and Jerry were already seated, and was asked to make himself comfortable.

Duncan commenced by fumbling in his desk drawer, Jerry lit a fag, and Ray drank the cold slops from someone's cup, which hadn't been cleared away from the previous day. Drawing some crumpled papers from the drawer as if to give himself some confidence, Duncan opened the conference.

'Well, Farquhar, Mr Quid, Mr Squeeze and myself wish you to consider joining us in partnership starting 1st January next. We have, the three of us and our predecessor, Mr Chancer, worked very hard and long in the business which, by now, you have come to know. Each of us was once at your stage, and each of us was invited in succession to join the firm from the belief of our forebear that we would honour the trust, as well as the opportunity which partnership affords and implies. We are all links in a chain,' he droned on, 'links in a chain stretching far into the past and far into the future. None of us three can go on forever, and it is for us to ensure, through involving young and enthusiastic blood like yourself, that the future is well secured. Without going into the details of what this would entail in money terms, what is your first reaction to joining with us, Farquhar?'

Farquhar didn't indulge any thinking time. He saw the tape, and was about to breast it.

'I'm very honoured, gentlemen. I feel very flattered to be considered for the team. I only hope I can attain and maintain the high standards which you gentlemen have set. My answer is yes – thanks.'

High standards be blowed, thought Farquhar – my brain could eat all three of theirs for breakfast and still be starving by lunchtime. However, if a little flattery is all that's needed to seal the bargain, a little flattery they would get.

'Splendid!' chorused the three gents.

'Now about money, Farquhar,' Duncan continued 'It's hard to be precise. You will get a share of profits over and above your salary, but how much this means depends on what's in the kitty at the end of your first year. We'd like to think that you would trust us to keep you right. After all, we are each in the same boat and none of us knows what is in store for us year by year. Suffice to say that Joe Public hasn't let us down so far!'

'That's OK by me, sir,' lied Farquhar, who was content at this stage to get his foot in the door. He could push it open as wide as he liked once over the threshold.

'I think this calls for a celebration party,' enthused Ray, as he did about anything likely to involve refreshment.

'Good idea, Mr Squeeze,' responded Duncan. 'Perhaps we can close the office about noon on 31st December and have the whole staff toast our new partner's health and prosperity.'

'Till about 4 o'clock?' smiled Jerry.
'Till the well runs dry,' beamed Duncan.
'I'd like to buy the wine as a token of my appreciation,' announced Farquhar.
'Wouldn't hear of it, my son,' growled Duncan good naturedly. 'Mr Squeeze wants to do the honours!'
'Me?' choked Ray, wiping his nose with his sleeve.
'Only joking, Ray – the firm will pay. It's a business meeting, so it's a business expense and will be tax-deductible.'
'Better get in a few bottles of spirits too, then,' said Ray, reviving. 'We can always take the spares home and drink the health of the Inspector of Taxes!'
'None of that kind of talk in front of the boy,' quipped Jerry. 'How about some coffee right now for starters – your treat, Farquhar.'
Mr Pickforth dialled for four coffees, and during the twenty minutes spent in drinking and chatting, Farquhar was for the first time party to the kind of conversation which hitherto had been indulged in by the three older ones alone. He became even less impressed with their acumen as he saw them with their guards down, and correspondingly more sure of himself. What he didn't realise at the time was that, in getting surer of himself for no good reason, he was getting more like the other three by the minute!
The word of Farquhar's promotion got round the office like a bushfire, courtesy of what Miss Bottoms had heard whilst dispensing the celebratory coffee. Lotte left for an early lunch in tears, bemoaning her lot as an older and more experienced candidate for partnership cursed for being female. 'Male pigs!' she muttered as she slid her long legs into her Mini and drove to the Queens Hotel for a solo lunch. Not wishing to face anyone she might know in the lounge, she went straight into the elegant dining room, having ordered a large gin and tonic at reception. She ordered a second from the wine waiter whilst waiting for her smoked salmon starter, and a third before her main course. She didn't see Farquhar coming into the dining room with pint in hand, nor did he know of her distraught state. But, in an instant, his shadow fell over her napkin, and Lotte looked up, moist-eyed and sad.

'Lotte – what's wrong?' asked Farquhar with real concern.

'Congratulations,' sobbed Lotte. 'I really am very happy for you, but I had thought that, perhaps, I too might have been considered.'

'Oh dear,' said Farquhar kindly, placing his free hand on her left shoulder. 'I hadn't thought of how you'd feel. How insensitive of me. Indeed I had really wanted to tell you myself.'

'That's all right, Farquhar. It's not your fault that I am just a female.'

'I'm jolly glad that you are, Lotte. You have more to be proud of than all the partners in the world.'

Farquhar sat down opposite Lotte without the need for invitation, and the couple held hands across the table. They didn't notice the waiter, pad in hand, waiting for Farquhar's order. Not knowing the extent of Lotte's prior intake, Farquhar ordered sole mornay for himself and a bottle of champagne to mark his special occasion.

Not wishing to dampen Farquhar's obvious excitement, Lotte did her duty by the champagne, feeling, surprisingly, better as the result – for a while anyway. The couple giggled their way through whatever of their meal was actually eaten, and Lotte finished her third gin over coffee. It was when Farquhar was paying the bill that she tried to stand up, and found that the walls of the hotel were rotating. Farquhar helped the young lady to his own car and drove her back to the office, and took a particularly attentive interest in her throughout the afternoon, barring all entries to her room and serving an endless chain of black coffee.

By 5.30 p.m., when the hubbub of business had ceased, the couple left by the back door, and Farquhar took his somewhat fragile – but much revived – colleague back to the hotel to re-claim her abandoned Mini. She got home safely, but the evening hangover left her thoroughly miserable, and a grim depression pervaded the Treacle household.

Farquhar spent the evening at a lecture on Law Reform and mixed easily with solicitors many years his senior – something he'd have found impossible only a few hours before.

The other saps – Smile, Quid and Squeeze – engaged themselves in less academic pursuits. Ray was the last of these three into his bed, feeling much as Lotte had done in the afternoon.

THE CHRISTMAS SPIRIT

Mid-December saw the first of the winter's snows. Just a few inches, nothing serious. Sufficient to garland even the ugliest parts of town with a tinsel beauty – and enough to delay Ray's arrival at work till nearer eleven. Though Duncan lived within walking distance of business, he didn't turn up at all on the first day of the snow. He phoned in about noon and spoke of his gout playing up, and could Lotte call at his house with his briefcase containing the day's mail and 'anything else lying on my desk or the floor nearby'. Jerry was in at work at his usual time, but left for lunch at 11.30 a.m. 'in case the roads got worse'. Of course the roads didn't get worse – they hadn't been bad at all – and mid-morning sanding had transformed all except side-roads into dirty wet channels.

Why tell you those things? Well – as Christmas approaches – law offices tend to quieten down. (Remember, this is still the nineteen-seventies!) Interest in the festive season overhauls interest in legal matters as a priority – and this is a priority in which even lawyers become involved. Partners vanish for hours on end to engage in Christmas shopping, or to accept lunch invitations from Banks, Building Societies, Insurance Brokers and others with the cash to spend on seasonal hospitality. The seasonal holidays start about tenth December, and even such a modest fall of snow is enough to advance further the Christmas spirit, with formerly dead trees and shrubbery – and condemned buildings – looking like a scene from a Scandinavian calendar. The only business interest taken by Chancers' top men involves inspection of the firms private ledgers to see how much has been earned – and how much of this has already been spent. There is a ritual about examination of the figures, with Duncan, Jerry and Ray huddled behind a closed door pouring over the relevant items.

'How on earth do you get through all that money, Ray? You certainly don't spend that much at your tailors!' observed Jerry.

'Bloody cheek,' snapped Ray. 'This is an office, not a fashion house. Anyway, this suit is only six years old, and if you buy good in the first place it should last.'

Now, this makes good sense to Ray, who feels vindicated, from the words of his own mouth. It doesn't however, explain the stains down his lapels or the fact that his right-hand jacket pocket is ripped, or the frayed turn-ups on his geriatric trousers

'No comment,' replied Jerry, lighting a fag.

'Easy to see where your money goes, Quid – it's all these cigarettes and your fancy holidays abroad. Wouldn't be surprised if you have some other expensive vice over and above the vices we already know about!'

'Gentlemen!' interrupted Duncan. 'It's none of the business of any of us to know how the others spend their earnings. We seem to be doing satisfactorily, and that's the main thing. Now you'll have to excuse me. I've to go to the Cash and Carry to buy a new anorak for Doreen's Christmas.'

'Generous bugger,' muttered Ray as Duncan left 'I wouldn't have been surprised had he just got her old one re-quilted!'

'You're a fine one to talk,' recalled Jerry, 'it's not so long ago you were shopping around for a replacement pedal for that second-hand tin trike you bought for your daughter's Christmas.'

'You swine!' rasped Ray, getting angry. 'Are you suggesting that I'm mean or something? If so you'd better come right out with it. I look after my family a bloody sight better than you do – but that'll surprise no one. By the time you have got yourself all ponced up with a suit for each hour of the day, it's no wonder you've damn-all left to spend on anyone else!'

'Calm down, son,' smiled Jerry, 'I had no idea you were so self-conscious about your meanness. You really shouldn't leave your copy of the local paper open on your desk with rings round items in 'Articles for Sale'. I see it's a Doll's House this year!'

'You bastard!!' yelled Ray, stamping out and banging the door. He re-entered almost at once.

'No, YOU get out, Quid, this is MY room!'

As already hinted, the Christmas spirit is on the march.

The staff also fall victim to mysterious absences on the run-up to Christmas. Most of them declare that they have 'a day or two' of their summer holiday entitlement still to come, and from about 18th December onwards only a skeleton staff remains. The few fly ones who take their 'day or two' between Christmas and New Year contrive the best part of a fortnight off, weekends included. And the traditional eight-hour day suffers contraction this side of January 5th. Only Miss Nockersby sticks to her task. And a good thing she does. Without her, the street door might as well stay locked.

'The clients should just hand their money in and leave us in peace,' pronounced Ray on 22nd whilst chatting to Miss Nockersby and filling his wallet from the Cash Desk.

'Let ME count what you're taking, Mr Squeeze!' she rasped. 'It's a big enough job balancing the cash at night without you lot dipping the till unsupervised.'

Ray handed over the money sheepishly.

Dipping her right forefinger into a moistened sponge, the Cashier studiously counted off the notes one by one, and handed the ten pounds to Ray.

'Now sign for it whilst I've got you in my sights,' she directed.

Ray signed.

'That's me off now to do my Christmas shopping, Miss Nockersby,' announced Ray as he slung his grimy sheepskin over his shoulder and headed for the door.

'There'll be plenty of change off ten pounds!' winked the cashier to Mrs Plum as the door swung shut behind their boss.

The Christmas holidays were very much family affairs for Messrs Smile, Quid and Squeeze. At least, nothing is chronicled about what they got up to. During the three days the office was open before the onset of the New Year Holidays, snow – which had obligingly fallen towards midnight on Christmas Eve – lay, then thawed, then fell again, followed by hard frost on 31st. Roads, footpaths and much else were like skating rinks, and plumbers got ready for a predictable bonanza during the holiday period, when stricken house holders would pay just about anything for help to avert disaster.

HOGMANAY

Hogmanay – and the New Year Party – got under way somewhat earlier than planned. The booze and canapés – specially the booze – had been delivered by Duncan's wine merchant the afternoon preceding. And it was barely ten o'clock in the morning when Ray volunteered to uncrate the hired glasses and 'check that they are clean'. It was but a small progression from doing this that the wine should also be sampled.

'Better come and help me, Jerry,' announced Ray through the former's ever-open door. 'We can't ply Farquhar with rotten drink on this important occasion. I think we should do some sampling, just to be on the safe side!'

Jerry needed no encouragement, and the two of them met Duncan on the way to the 'Rest Room' in which the goodies had been deposited.

'You're the *real* wine expert, Duncan,' smiled Ray. 'You'd better lend us your finely-tuned palate.'

'I'm far too busy,' lied Duncan. The others winked at each other and walked on. Duncan followed, as they knew he would.

Ray was the first to raise a glass of dark heavy red wine up to the light, more to savour the moment than to check for sediment.

'God! Not red wine at this time of day!' exclaimed Jerry. 'It's bad enough having a headache late evening without asking for one mid-morning.'

'Piffle!' cheered Ray, as he slurped the contents of the glass with the thirst of a desert explorer. In fairness, half the wine spilled down his tie. 'Better try the white, then the rosé whilst the taste-buds are discerning enough to tell the difference.'

Whilst Ray gulped samples of each colour Duncan nosed his way round the selection, half-moon glasses perched on the point of his sniffing equipment, but allowing none of the wine to pass his lips.

'I have two Brethren ladies from the Gospel Hall coming in at eleven. Don't think it would be good form to breathe strong drink all over them,' explained Duncan.

'Might make them jealous,' sniggered Ray, half-drinking and half-spilling his fifth glass. 'I see we have some spirits here too, boys – can we be sure that even they are up to standard without checking?'

'Leave these bloody spirits alone, Ray,' warned Jerry, still fumbling with the Bacardi and tonic which he had poured for himself at the outset

'I see you've found the rum all right, mate. I think I should test the gin. You know how easily gin can go off in a sealed bottle!'

Whereupon Ray stretched his arm out towards the litre of Gordons.

'Put that down, you idiot,' snapped Duncan. 'Get that Bottoms woman to get coffee on tap and keep your hands off the liquor till after I have opened the proceedings.'

'But that'll be nearly two hours yet,' simpered Ray, huffily.

'Well you can bloody wait, then,' Duncan ordered unsympathetically.

There are times when Duncan gives instructions and everyone does the opposite for their own good. There are other times when Duncan gives instructions and it is instinctively known that he must be obeyed. This was one such time, and the 'Rest Room' was vacated by all three. But not before Ray had emptied his glass, as well as two of the glasses which Duncan had sniffed.

Duncan was barely back in his room when Zoë phoned to say that Mrs and Miss Drinkwater were in the waiting room. When the ladies were shown in, the lawyer greeted them both with a bonhomie, which stretched his hypocrisy to its well-extended limit.

'How nice to see you both. You do indeed look well, no doubt inspired by your Christmastide devotions.'

'Thank you, Mr Smile,' replied the Drinkwaters in unison, stretching their thin white lips into something approaching a smile of their own, then re-pokerfacing as if ashamed of looking other than serious. Dressed all in black, with ashen faces, unadorned by anything more cosmetic than the afterglow of lifebuoy and a scrubber, the Drinkwater persons clearly carried their asceticism to full measure.

'What can I have the pleasure of doing for you then?'

The words were out of his mouth before he had time to consider that the mention of 'pleasure' may have been construed as something obscene.

He even felt uneasy about his own surname in such sombre company.

'Well it's like this, Mr Smile, the people next door to us in the big house – you know, the ones who do bed and breakfast – well, they've applied for a drink licence.' This was the older lady.

'How awful!' replied Duncan, biting his lip.

'We ARE glad you agree, Mr Smile, because we want you to put a stop to it. First it will be a glass of wine at the table, then a bar, then orgies and sex and things – and the whole area will become a suburb of Sodom and Gomorrah.'

Mrs Drinkwater's face became grotesquely contorted as she spat out her dreaded prediction.

'Oh surely not, Mrs Drinkwater. Have you not thought it just as likely that the conduct of those next door will be as readily influenced by the goodness which shines out of your own windows? If good and evil are living next door to each other, why is it that you think the evil will triumph over the good? Surely we are taught that it is good which triumphs over evil!'

'You know, we hadn't thought of it that way,' said the younger of the two. 'What you mean is that we shouldn't object to the drink licence but should ask God's help to keep business away from the rotten place?'

'Not exactly, Miss Drinkwater. What I mean is that in however dreadful a manner the next-door people conduct themselves, your role is to shine brightly in the midst of the darkness, whatever shape or form that darkness may take. Your goodness will be far more prominent next to an Inn than it could ever be next to a Cathedral. And look at all the treasure you will store up for yourselves in Heaven by being brave amid adversity here on earth.'

At the mention of 'treasure' the ladies looked noticeably cheerier.

'Thank you very much for your wise words, Mr Smile. We shall do as you say, and gird ourselves with prayer.'

'Amen,' pronounced Duncan as he rose and bowed the Drinkwaters out his door.

When they had gone, Duncan said to himself aloud, 'I could go that drink now all right,' knowing that he, Duncan, was solicitor to the

Drinkwaters' neighbour and on whose behalf he had sponsored the licensing application.

Needless to say, while Duncan was engaged, Ray had been helping the ladies of the staff to set up the bar in the 'Rest Room', at the same time sampling the gin just to be on the safe side. By noon, he had taken on a rosy glow; the front of his suit was covered in damp stains and Miss Bottoms had been sent out for a box of Havanas. Even the staff members who had taken days off turned up to join the others for the Hogmanay Party and the full complement of Chancers' personnel, by 12.30 p.m. ringed the extremities of the room like wallflowers at a children's' party.

Lotte presided over the savouries, Ray over the drink with Farquhar at his elbow, Miss Nockersby twittered on about the cash not yet being balanced and about business lost by virtue of the street-door's early closure. Paul Snotty lurked in a corner behind Miss Bottoms who, for her part, looked like someone who knew her posterior was about to be felt, and who was ready to strike hard if it was. Eunice, Chi-Chi and Rachel, Ethel, Sandy and Darky sat in a row ready for the action to start. Jerry and Duncan stood, hands behind their backs like the Duke of Edinburgh, the latter thus concealing the notes for his speech. The hum of conversation was embarrassed awkward and artificial. Jerry went over and closed the door, and Duncan stepped into the middle of the room, applied his spectacles, dabbed his nose with the back of his hand, and spoke.

'Ladies and Gentlemen, it is not every day that it's the thirty first of December ...'

Stirring stuff.

'Nor is it every day that we assume a new partner into our firm.'

'Hear! Hear!' Ray interjected, amidst titters, fiddling with the gin bottle.

'Today is the thirty first of December and we are assuming Farquhar Pickforth as a partner at Chancers...'

Mock surprise and gasping from the listeners.

'... And we are gathered together to join in welcoming Farquhar into our company and to wish him – and all of you – a very Happy New Year and prosperous and Happy New Years to follow.'

Jerry thought he had finished and was getting his hands ready to clap when Duncan continued.

'Partnership is an honourable estate. It carries privileges, be assured. But it also carries weighty responsibilities. Why, when I was Farquhar's age, I was young healthy and lean. Nothing was too much trouble for me. It is not the privileges of partnership which have wrought the change in me. Be assured however, that responsibilities take their toll, and you, Farquhar, must accept that partnership, like marriage, is for better of for worse. I hope that your health will rise above the worries and that your blood pressure, unlike mine, behaves itself into contented old age. Now I don't expect you want to hear me talking all day …'

'Too bloody right' slurred Ray.

'I'll ignore Mr Squeeze's interruption,' said Duncan sternly. 'I'll just finish by repeating my most sincere good wishes to you all. You'll pardon me if I leave shortly. I haven't been feeling too well, and shall just have a small drink with you to be sociable and in the hope of settling my stomach.'

Duncan bowed, took two steps backwards and re-joined Jerry amid polite clapping. It took only a couple of minutes to see that everyone had a full glass, then Jerry said simply,

'To Farquhar!'

All drank enthusiastically and wired into the savouries, which Lotte handed round quite beautifully, attentively smoothing her hair and her skirt with her spare hand.

With barely a chance to swallow more than a couple of mouthfuls, Farquhar stepped forward and spoke, so interrupting the blur of freshly initiated chatter.

'Friends,' he said. 'I feel deeply honoured to have been invited into partnership. I would like to express my warm thanks to my senior partners for their confidence, which I promise to honour at all times. I'd like to thank all the staff for your loyalty and industry. Never hesitate to share your ideas and your problems with me. I may be young, but I assure you that nothing will be too much trouble for me, and my door will always be open if there's anything you want to discuss. Enjoy your wine. Enjoy the party, and let's enjoy working together – but not till after the New Year. And a very good New Year to you all.'

Duncan, who believed that whisky would be kinder to his stomach than any of the acidic wines on offer, sat beside Miss Nockersby with his second glass. The warm glow had eased his stomach-nerves and his face coloured richly as he chatted animatedly, feeling much better.

Ray, cigar in hand and waving his arms about like a windmill – spitting more gin in the process as he chatted incoherently with a glazed grin – sent Snotty round the office to check that all plugs were disconnected for the holiday period, then promptly took over the apprentice's space next to Miss Bottoms.

'Well Virginia, how are you enjoying working here?'

Miss Bottoms tried to ease back from the various smells, which emanated from Ray's breath, but the wall barred her escape.

'Oh everything is OK, sir,' she replied nervously, watching Ray's arm reach for the wall behind her head for support. He lurched forward and his face brushed against her hair. 'And how is Mrs Squeeze?' she enquired.

Ray grimaced and removed his left hand.

'Very well indeed, Virginia. But I didn't come here to talk about Marjory.'

'What did you come to talk about then, sir?'

'I thought you could help me to tidy up the store-room for half an hour before we leave. We could take a bottle and glasses with us to make the task less irksome.'

'PARDON?' exclaimed the girl.

'Wheesht, my dear,' he swayed. 'We don't want the others to hear, do we?'

'I shouldn't imagine *you* want anyone to hear, Mr Squeeze,' said Virginia loudly, catching the attention of the extended ears of Eunice and Darky.

'What did you say, Ginny?' enquired Eunice.

'I was just telling Miss Bottoms that the store-room could do with a face-lift.' Ray chipped in, beads of sweat standing proud all over his face. '...and she offered to do it now – but, of course, I wouldn't hear of it.'

Easing himself out of the jam of his own making, Ray hid his embarrassment in a topped-up drink, and started to hiccup uncontrollably.

'Filthy bastard,' muttered Miss Bottoms as she turned to tell 'les girls' what Ray had been up to. Their conversation became lost in the increasing clamour as empty bottles overflowed from plastic wastebinliners.

Jerry handed round his cigarettes, knowing that only two of the staff smoked. He lost fifteen in one round and didn't repeat the performance.

'Didn't know you smoked,' he said to Darky.

'Well, I don't really, Mr Quid, but it is a special occasion, and it's not every day I get the offer. Any offer! Is Mr Smile all right?'

Both looked for, and found Duncan sniggering at something funny he'd said to Yolande Nockersby. Yolande had one hand over her mouth to prevent her mirthful teeth from flying out and the other on a full tumbler of red wine. They had their arms round each other's shoulders.

'I can't imagine what they're laughing about, Darky. The only funny thing that happens here is how there's enough money to pay everyone.'

Darky straightened up. 'PAY! – Do you call what we get pay? More like slave labour that's what! Don't you agree, girls?'

As Darky turned to focus on her work-mates, she staggered, and Jerry noticed that the poor soul was drunk.

'Bugger it!' mimed Jerry. 'It's our own bloody fault. Lash out some cash for a party, and the swine drink up then tell you what they really think of you.' He slid out of the group and humphed off to the silence and contemplative safety of his room. Shoving open the door to his refuge, he found Ray with his hand inside Chi-Chi's blouse, reversed out, phoned for his wife and waited on the freezing kerbside till she arrived to drive him home.

At just after four o'clock, the party wound up. Exchanging greetings and kisses, the throng erupted on to the ice-bound pavement and, arm-in-arm, cascaded linked together into the gutter where they settled like the contents of an upturned dustbin. Two police constables, having a smoking break in a nearby doorway, diplomatically turned in the opposite direction and disappeared into the now dense snowfall.

Duncan broke his wrist. Ray was upended on his hip, smashing the gin-bottle secreted in his coat pocket and, more importantly, losing the remaining quarter of its contents down his leg. However, he bravely offered to drive Duncan to the hospital, an offer which Duncan undiplomatically declined rather than be an accessory to another inevitable accident. Ray was displeased as spurned inebriates tend to be, and a scuffle ensued as the pleasurable (to him) result of which he again fell to nestle beside Miss Bottoms at the kerbside. She grabbed his car-keys and dropped them down the adjacent drain and, by doing so, probably saved Ray from a New Year in the nick.

Duncan re-entered the office with difficulty and much publicised pain, ordered an ambulance for himself and taxis enough to barrow the remainder of the shambles home. Once back from Out-Patients and well doctored with pain-killers, Duncan attended a church service to bring in the New Year. He gave generously, for him, to the collection for underprivileged Africans, went to bed at 1 a.m. after toasting Doreen's New Year health in Horlicks, and wakened to a sunny first January feeling fine – but feigning just enough ill-health to be excused helping Doreen prepare for the family's arrival for New Year's dinner.

Ray's Hogmanay taxi had taken him from the office to the golf club for a blurred session with 'the boys' and to top up his artificial euphoria before going home to face Marjory. He wakened at noon the day following feeling hellish. The sunshine helped a little and, the word being that bits of the course may be open for play, his recovery gathered speed.

When Anne and Jerry got home, they had a mug of soup at around 5 p.m., after which he dosed through the evening hours – the best way of watching Hogmanay television – then they toasted each other and the New Year by the light of their roaring log fire.

'You've told me about Duncan and Ray carrying on at the party, pet. What about yourself? Am I supposed to believe that you were the model gentleman throughout?'

'Not really, honey,' blushed Jerry. 'But you don't really expect me to go into the detail of my own appalling conduct, do you?'

'Why ever not, Jerry?'

'Because this is MY story, Anne, and I feel entitled to tell it my way.'

'Do you think anyone will ever read all this nonsense?'

'We'll have to wait and see,' mused Jerry.

EPILOGUE

THE NEW ORDER

The arrival of Margaret Thatcher's Conservative Government had her hell-bent on promoting free enterprise in every corner of her domain, which looked like comforting news for self-employed entrepreneurians. However, firstly in England and Wales, then into Scotland, came the push to erode so-called monopolies of handling certain aspects of business, including the handling of property conveyancing by solicitors. In her wisdom, the Prime Minister had been behind the removal of opticians' monopoly of providing optical services to the extent that just about any idiot could acquire a job-lot of spectacles and set up in competition with highly skilled practitioners of thirty or more years' standing – almost solely on the basis of whose services were cheaper. Excellent news for the idiot, but not such good news for the opticians – nor for the country's eyesight.

Something similar appears to have been in Mrs Thatcher's mind for legal practitioners. After all, anyone can do conveyancing (a popular misconception) so why shouldn't lawyers be exposed to competition with non-lawyers for the handling of this lucrative aspect of legal practice. Competition is healthy and brings down costs was the Government's simplistic assumption. Damn-all about who's best, most careful, most thorough, most competent, helpful or courteous or whose services are most comprehensive, and long-term. Just who's cheapest!

Lawyers were called upon to give estimates before starting a job. Fair enough for roofing contractors and coachbuilders who get a chance to examine the mess before costing its repair. But lawyers were required to quote fees for the transfer of property without having the chance of seeing any of the paperwork until AFTER they had nominated their proposed fee-charge.

Great, thought the lawyers. What next? Free competition in brain surgery? Or, when comfortably strapped into your jet plane en route for the Caribbean, do you really want to hear:

'This is your Captain, Norman Finn. You'll probably remember me. I'm usually the butcher at the Co-op but I had this notion to drive a plane and was prepared to do it a lot cheaper than the regular driver....'

To a man, Duncan, Ray and Jerry shrank from the idea of advertising and, indeed, from any change in their comfortably established order of things. None of them was too old to adapt, but each of them was too old to *want* to adapt under duress in new circumstances the wisdom of which they genuinely challenged.

'How can we afford to cut charges to compete and still pay rising overheads and keep our incomes up?' despaired Duncan.

'You bloody can't!' sneered Ray. 'And the bigger fool you are if you try. We're all in the same boat, so not a bloody lawyer in Scotland can afford to pull the plug on himself! Just charge as you've always done, and no one will notice the difference.'

'What about the youngsters setting up now, who'll do anything to get their share of the market – they're bound to make inroads and skin some of our share,' moaned Duncan.

'Would you want to be one of them, Mr Smile? If so, feel free to set up on your own and test the water. NOW if you want!' was Ray's unhelpful response.

Jerry had sat in silence, puffing at a fag.

'I don't like it.' He offered.

'You too, Mr Quid?' shot Ray 'Well you know what you lily-livered girls can do, don't you! Be assured when you cowards have slunk off there'll be tons of gravy for me – and to spare. So make up your minds – do we fire ahead and RAISE our charges and to hell with it, or do you two pansies run away from Thatcher's paper pellets?'

'But,' said Duncan, 'doesn't the Law Society say we'd better follow Government's requirements or even worse measures will be forced on us?'

'Bugger the Law Society,' was Ray's immediate response, without any expressed reason. Then, after a pause, he added,

'The Law Society doesn't have an office in Piddletown. The Law Society doesn't have any clients here, any staff here, any computers, typewriters, accounting machines or any books to balance. The Law Society doesn't have our bloody overdraft, families to support – NOR does our clientele have a clue what the Law Society is, nor does it care. Whether or not we make our living is up to us, not up to the Law Society. So I suggest that you get back to your own bloody rooms this very minute and, starting at 'A' through to 'Z' go through your bloody cabinets file by file and check how many dozens of jobs each of you has done and not charged for. I bet you have a good fortnight ahead of each of you sending out bills which in total could set us up damn-near to bloody retirement!!'

Duncan and Jerry were stunned. Never had they heard Ray rattle on quite so near-eloquently and barely stopping for breath. The only sensible thing for the two of them to have done was to leave, but as Jerry turned to do so, Duncan foolishly took on the pose of elder statesman.

'It has been a tradition at Chancers,' he opened 'that we should always show a willingness to offer counsel without thought of reward, and frequently for nothing. You have no idea how much goodwill is engendered by my gratuitous advices …'

Ray turned white, and interrupted, 'Good God, man! Gratuitous advices! Goodwill my buttocks! While you are mumbling your useless gratuitous advices I am breaking my back doing PAID work so that you can spend money on yourself like a man with ten hands. Well, I'm not having it – not me! Quid can pay for your bloody extravagances, but count me out. Start earning big money for this firm NOW, Mr Smile, or take you and your bloody goodwill down these stairs and don't come back!!'

Duncan started shaking and sweating.

'Aren't you being a little hasty, Raymond?'

'I've never until now seen a man who can shake and sweat to order,' continued Ray. 'The Old Vic would be proud to welcome you to the boards – away and suck a couple of placebos and take an unaccustomed early afternoon off – and be here sharp at 11 a.m. tomorrow if you want to remain one of us.'

Ray's face had softened to a gruesome grin, and Duncan felt the dampness on his back dry into his shirt as the situation defused.

'I think I'll do the 'A' to 'Z' in my filing cabinets,' cowed Jerry, who had stood inert in the doorway for ten minutes.

'There's a good boy, Jerry!' winked Ray. 'I might even do something similar myself.'

'Good old Maggie Thatcher,' concluded Duncan. 'Maybe her damn-fool nonsense has awakened us to an efficiency we've lacked.'

'An efficiency YOU have lacked, Mr Smile,' frowned Jerry.

Ignoring this as if deaf, Duncan edged towards the door.

'We'll start tomorrow, then, shall we?' he winked.

Farquhar missed out on these exchanges, being out for lunch with Lotte. Even already he had decided that partnership harmony is best served by being elsewhere when its affairs are under discussion. And, in any event, what had he to learn from these idiots?

It didn't seem to occur to him that by these, his own thoughts and deeds, there were ample signs that he had already been 'contaminated', and that the seeds of his own absorption into the ways of Potty Chambers had already been well and truly sown!